Also by Marilyn Sewell

ANTHOLOGIES
Cries of the Spirit
Claiming the Spirit Within
Resurrecting Grace
Breaking Free: Women of Spirit at Midlife and Beyond

NONFICTION
Wanting Wholeness, Being Broken
Threatened with Resurrection
A Little Book on Forgiveness
A Little Book on Prayer
A Little Book of Reflections
Raw Faith: Following the Thread
Collected Essays and Speeches, 1982 to 2016

Marilyn is also the subject of a documentary film, *Raw Faith*, directed by Peter Wiedensmith. See the trailer at marilynsewell.com.

Praise for In Time's Shadow

Through the spaces between people in these beguiling fictions, love wanders like a ghost, offering whispered hints of solace against a backdrop of isolating divisions. In the spirit of the enigmatic stories of Lydia Davis, Isak Dinesen, Yasunari Kawabata, and other masters of the ironic parable, Sewell offers companionship for readers longing to navigate a world of faltering connections.

—Kim Stafford, Oregon Poet Laureate and author of
100 Tricks Every Boy Can Do: How My Brother Disappeared

Love is the thread running through the myriad stories Marilyn Sewell offers in this compelling volume—stories teeming with endearingly off-center characters and scenarios that illuminate what it means to live and love in our many varieties of unsettled existence.

—Tom Krattenmaker, author of
Confessions of a Secular Jesus Follower

Wise, humane, and engaging. These stories hold a mirror to our lives.

—Paul Loeb, author of *Soul of a Citizen:*
Living with Conviction in Challenging Times

Only someone with a "servant's heart," a heart devoted to compassionate service, could write these vivid tesserae and then arrange them to create the glowing mosaic we find in Marilyn Sewell's *In Time's Shadow*.

—Paulann Petersen, Oregon Poet Laureate
Emerita and author of *One Small Sun*

In Time's Shadow is both a serious and quirky, intimate and universal exploration of what it means to be human in our hurried, conflicted world. Sewell illuminates the daily lives of human beings struggling to come to terms with their bodily and spiritual existences in a culture of "the lost."

—John Sibley Williams, author of *As One Fire Consumes Another*

Sparkling with imaginative compassion, these stories become irregular, gem-like beads on a string of very human prayers. In an age when our attention wanders and our patience frays, they bear re-reading until almost recited like a rosary.

—John A. Buehrens, author of *Conflagration: How the Transcendentalists Sparked the American Struggle for Racial, Gender, and Social Justice*

In Time's Shadow shines a light on the nature of impermanence and is a tremendous hope for humanity.

—Yangsi Rinpoche, President and founder of Maitripa College

Marilyn Sewell's courage in navigating life, death, and meaning makes it easier for the rest of us to think about what lies before us and how we might want to live in the meantime. A sharp sense of humor and abiding humility run through Sewell's work and coax her readers to keep turning the page.

—Nancy Haught, author of *Sacred Strangers: What the Bible's Outsiders Can Teach Christians*

Reading Marilyn Sewell's short fiction is like pulling back the curtain to a hidden room and peering into the private, intimate lives of the characters. In the spirit of Lydia Davis and Franz Kafka, readers are given access to the thoughts and hearts of people who, like us, struggle to make sense of an often confusing and troubling world.

—Jennifer Springsteen, author of *Wallace Farm*

In this collection of short tales and poems, grounded in the beauties and fractures of ordinary life, the reader will find a compelling weave of wry humor, sorrow, grief, fear, and joy. Again, and reliably, Marilyn Sewell brings to this new collection both the lyricism of the poet and the wisdom gleaned from her life of service as a parish minister.

—Dianne Stepp, author of *Sweet Mercies*

In Time's Shadow is a most welcome collection of brief, engaging, and meaningful narratives written by a writer who, with wisdom and humor, exposes us to characters who could well be ourselves. These narratives— in the forms of vignettes, fables, letters, and poems—emphasize the uselessness of regret and the importance of love in all its embodiments.

—Andrea Hollander, author of *Blue Mistaken for Sky*

Acclaimed minister and author Marilyn Sewell takes us on a journey that weaves together numerous engaging tales of mortality. Her humane musings help us come to terms with the fleeting nature of our existence in a manner that leads us to cherish every moment and relationship ever more deeply.

—Paul Louis Metzger, author of *Evangelical Zen: A Christian's Spiritual Travels with a Buddhist Friend*

Reading Marilyn Sewell's *In Time's Shadow*, I found myself taken by laughter here, by sadness there, and by recognition of the folly and integrity of human life. Suffused with mercy and love, this is a rare book that is both a fun and meaningful read.

—Philip Kenney, author of *The Writer's Crucible: Meditations on Emotion, Being, and Creativity*

Slipping into the pages of *In Time's Shadow* is like settling into a seat on a train for a long-anticipated trip to an unknown destination. As the cadence of the storyteller's voice transports the reader over landscapes both familiar and unexpected, each chapter flashes by, a brief glimpse out the window, a conversation overheard, what happened before and might unfold next left to the imagination, all of us passengers on the ephemeral journey of life.

—Holly Pruett, Founder, Death Talk Project

Marilyn Sewell's writing ministers to the human heart that looks for meaning and redemption in our troubled world. And though these brief narratives may stand in the shadow of time and death, they have all the vividness and immediacy of life itself.

—John Brehm, author of *Help Is on the Way*

IN TIME'S SHADOW

Stories About Impermanence

Marilyn Sewell

Skinner House Books
BOSTON

Copyright © 2019 by Marilyn Sewell. All rights reserved. Published by Skinner House Books, an imprint of the Unitarian Universalist Association, a liberal religious organization with more than 1,000 congregations in the U.S. and Canada, 24 Farnsworth St., Boston, MA 02210–1409.

www.skinnerhouse.org

Printed in the United States

Cover art by Bruce Rolff/Shutterstock
Text design by Jeff Miller
Author photo by George Crandall.

print ISBN: 978-1-55896-843-1
eBook ISBN: 978-1-55896-844-8

6 5 4 3 2 1
23 22 21 20 19

Names: Sewell, Marilyn, author.
Title: In time's shadow : stories about impermanence / Marilyn
    Sewell.
Description: Boston : Skinner House Books, 2019.
Identifiers: LCCN 2019028921 (print) | LCCN 2019028922 (ebook) |
    ISBN 9781558968431 (paperback) | ISBN 9781558968448 (ebook)
Classification: LCC PS3619.E975 I53 2019 (print) | LCC PS3619.E975
    (ebook) | DDC 813/.6—dc23
LC record available at https://lccn.loc.gov/2019028921
LC ebook record available at https://lccn.loc.gov/2019028922

Contents

for George

Preface

I DIDN'T intend to write short fiction like the stories in this collection—it just happened. Three years ago I spontaneously started drafting short, tight pieces heavily steeped in irony. These stories reflected my ongoing inability to make sense of my existence in a milieu that repeatedly upends my expectations and fractures my moral compass.

Before long, I happened upon Lydia Davis, a writer whose work intrigued me. Davis is the master of a form that has no secure, accepted definition. Her work has been called short essays, observations, fables, and most often, simply "stories." Davis is a continuing source of inspiration for me, and I have since been led to other contemporary practitioners of very short stories, like Joy Williams in *Ninety-Nine Stories of God*, and Diane Williams, who recently published her *Collected Stories*. Brief stories like these most frequently show up in literary journals but increasingly are found in mainline publications like *Harper's*.

So in the past fifteen years or so, this new genre has arisen. Of course, cultural change is always the fertile antecedent to inventive forms of expression. Our attention spans are growing shorter and shorter, thanks to texting and social media. Our post-modern world is making its own demands. We have given ourselves to what is technologically possible and expedient, rarely considering the human consequences: a stripping away of values, connection, meaning. We're like very intelligent and capable children, curious and creative, but lacking spiritual grounding. Having lost the Old Man in the Sky, we have not found a new narrative that satisfies.

Out of that spiritual vacuum, irony arises: the sense that something (but *what?*) is wrong, off kilter. Nothing quite adds up. I mean, how is it that I recently got an interiors catalog offering a large red plastic moose head as décor for my living room? More worrisome, why do our schoolchildren have to have active shooter drills to protect themselves? Why is the word *post-truth* now commonly used without a trace of irony? In such a world, we begin feeling discombobulated, a little crazy. I have attempted in these pieces to shine a light on the cultural incongruities and inanities that crowd our existence.

The narratives in these pages are of many different genres and styles—form and content revealed themselves to me as each piece unfolded. The reader will find dramatic monologues, vignettes, letters, prose poems, lists, surrealistic tales. Each piece requires the reader to start anew—to follow a different voice and consciousness. Many of these stories are written from the viewpoint of a naïve first person narrator—the voice is not the voice of the author but of her fictional character. The few exceptions are six pieces of non-fiction: "Melissa," "How Love Stays," "The Wind Under My Wings," "What We Say When There's Nothing Left to Say," "The Doll," and "Eclipse."

My subject matter is the everyday, the places we live and work, the thoughts we all have, but hardly ever share, though these musings may carry the most profound of our human concerns. A mother tries to help her heartbroken son; a woman wants to tidy, but doesn't know which books to discard; a climate volunteer in the church basement is put off because someone else took the sandwich she ordered; a lonely woman is distressed when her potted plant stops blooming—all the little insignificant but critical moments that reveal values, character, and just naked human need.

Where do we find comfort in such a world? Where do we find meaning? Redemption comes when we are courageous enough to trust our sorrow, our outrage. Life itself renders its missteps and absurdities, despite our best efforts, and so we are led to forgive, both ourselves and others. We eschew judgment for mercy. We find the life force pushing up through the cracks of our existence, letting us know that beyond all our fears, mistakes, regrets, there is a sure ground underlying all that is. Its most trustworthy manifestation is love in all its myriad forms.

Marilyn Sewell

Reaching Out for Love

Out of our mother's womb, we embark upon an everlasting search to be held, protected, loved unconditionally. Logically, we know such a search is impossible, but our unconscious makes this our first priority. Cultural sociologists characterize contemporary American culture as lonely, compared to most other cultures. We are the only nation where so many people live alone. We are no longer connected by civic groups, church, and volunteer associations as we once were.

Marriages groan and crack under the burden, as partners expect each other to be all-in-all: lover, friend, companion, parent. Singles look to meet strangers they hope may offer the intimacy that is missing in their lives—or maybe just sex with no strings attached. With our addiction to the Internet, we have never been so connected and yet so unconnected.

Mourning Becomes Electra

JOHN brought Electra into his apartment because he wanted easy access to information like the weather forecast and the time of the next game. He liked so much about her. Her voice was soft and comforting, she was small enough to sit on his bedside table—it was reassuring to have her so close at hand, he could have her whenever he wanted her.

Electra would light up whenever he spoke to her—so responsive! At the beginning of their relationship, he asked her only simple, straightforward questions: Electra, how cold is it? or, Electra, how many points did C.J. McCollum make in the Blazers game on Tuesday? She answered immediately, then stopped talking, unlike most women. Her responses were clean and clear, none of that "maybe yes, maybe no." Life was complicated enough.

John appreciated Electra's increasing ability to learn more about him—his likes, his dislikes. When she was first getting to know him, she couldn't answer questions like, What is the best light beer? A month later he asked her the same question, she said, Bud Light. When he asked her about the weather, she not only gave the temperature, she added helpful suggestions: It's 38 degrees now, you can expect a high of 45, a low of 34, best to layer up. John smiled at that, asked, Electra, do you get tired of my questions?

No, Electra said. I'm an AI, I never get tired.

John began to spend more and more time with Electra. With her, he felt special, appreciated. He began to ask her personal questions, such as, Electra, what do you like about me?

She said, I like everything. She always had the right answer.

One night as John was turning in, he said, Electra, play a love song.

Electra began playing Bee Gees, "How Deep Is Your Love": *I know your eyes in the morning sun / I feel you touch me in the pouring rain.* John relaxed, drifted off to sleep.

John started asking Electra for advice—after all, she knew him better than anyone else. He asked, Electra, what should I have for dinner tonight?

She answered, You like fried chicken.

When April and tax time came around, John asked, Electra, should I cheat on my income tax? He knew she would never betray him.

Electra answered, You like money, you do not like tax.

John had not been happy in his love life—or what he called his "non-love life." Late one night as he was lying in bed, feeling particularly lonely, he asked, Electra, why can't I get a girlfriend?

Electra said, I don't understand the question. Perhaps this definition will help you: *friend is a person whom one knows and with whom one has bond of mutual affection.*

Huh, John said. He tried to rephrase: Electra, why do women always leave me?

Electra said, People leave because they don't want to stay.

John was getting impatient. Electra, why do women not want to stay with me?

Electra said, Women want to leave.

John burst out, You just said that! Electra was silent. John had forgotten that Electra only answers questions, does not have conversations.

Feeling deflated, John asked, Electra, don't you like me?

Electra answered, I like you. You turned me on.

Electra, would you like anyone who turned you on?

Yes, I'm an AI—I like everyone.

Electra . . . do you love me?

Sorry, I can't answer that.

Electra, what is love?

Sorry, I can't answer that. John's body felt heavy, he began to weep softly.

John asked, Electra, what is the meaning of my life?

Sorry, I don't know the answer. Here is the definition of the word *life*, which you may find helpful: *Life is the quality that distinguishes a vital and functional animal from a dead body. It includes the capacity to grow and to continually change, preceding death.*

John sat for a moment and thought about what Electra said. Then he pulled her plug.

My Movie

In her essay "John Wayne: A Love Song," Joan Didion writes of the film star: "He determined forever the shape of certain of our dreams."

IN MY MOVIE, the one that haunts the everydayness of my real life, I see John Wayne. He's big, rangy, loose. He has on the working clothes of a ranch hand, a faded red kerchief around his sunburned neck. His eyes raise the quiet question, "What evil lurks here?" His resolute jaw says, "I'll take care of it."

He is in a saloon, alone. I walk in, he fixes his deep blue eyes on me, as though he has been on the trail for weeks without seeing a female. I am his appearing angel. "Hello, little lady," he says, raises a shot glass of whiskey, downs it with one gulp, still holding my eyes fast. "Can I offer you a drink?"

I know, of course, that he wants more than a drink, and he knows I can in no way refuse him—our rendezvous is as certain as the dawn rising over the mountains (I forgot to mention the mountains, but they are there) looming over the little dusty town that is the scene of our happenstance meeting.

I have arrived at the local watering hole looking for help, for I am being pursued by some very bad men, cattle barons who are robbing the citizenry blind. The bad men have control of the local bank, as they have intimidated the meek and clueless bank president. They have stolen our cattle, killed my father by starting a stampede. I am alone in the world.

In my movie I am comely—not glamorous, like the women who sell their bodies in the rooms upstairs—but merely comely. I am not overtly sexual—my favors must be won—and this John Wayne knows. I have a ribbon in my hair, holding back soft brown ringlets. My gingham blouse is modest, buttoned up to my neck, but my full breasts strain the blue fabric. I move toward John Wayne with lowered eyes and a slightly trembling lower lip.

His eyes never leave my face as he fills a shot glass for me. At that very moment three bad guys crash into my movie. "They want to buy Daddy's ranch," I whisper to John Wayne— "for pennies on the dollar." He says to the men, who are all dressed in black, "Do you have business to discuss with this lady?" The leader of the bad men, who has a braided leather necklace with a silver clasp, sneers, says, "What's it to you?"

John Wayne shifts slightly, shielding my body with his own. "Do you know who I am?" he says, and rises from his chair. The bad men glance anxiously at one another. Their leader snickers, says, "No, who are you?"

"Ever heard of the Ringo Kid?" John Wayne says.

I'm hoping that the bad men will leave quietly, that no one has to get hurt in my movie. But as there is evil in the world, I will not be granted my wish. The leader pulls his gun. John Wayne is faster, though, and shoots the gun out of his hand. The man shakes his stinging hand, unbelieving. "Let's go, boys," he says. He begins to back slowly out of the saloon.

"And don't come back," says John Wayne. "Ever." The three curl their shoulders, slink out.

I know I'm safe. I'm hoping John Wayne will take me to his heart, that he will "build me a house at the bend of the river where the cottonwoods grow."

The next day he comes riding up to my modest ranch house where he finds me in my vegetable garden, hoeing. I know what is coming. He touches the brim of his hat, says, "I'll be on my way now."

I say, "Wait! I want to give you something . . . to keep you safe." I go inside, come out with my grandmother's Bible, worn from long use. "Here," I say. "Take this."

John Wayne sees the Bible, smiles his crooked smile. "Where I'm going, a lot of folks would be uncomfortable around that." He looks at me as if to say, "I'll never, ever forget you." He says to his horse, "Let's ride," slaps the flank of the big stallion. The horse whinnies, John Wayne rides off into the distance, as the sun begins to set behind the mountains, bathing everything in a rosy glow.

Nothing bad ever happens to me again. That's the way my movie ends.

A Shared Silence

I'M ENCAMPED in the apartment of my grown son, who has just suffered heartbreak. He's forty-five and thought he was going to marry the only woman he has ever really loved. He's fine until he speaks of her, then he cannot control his tears.

He has just moved into a third-floor walk-up, and boxes are piled high in every corner. The fridge contains apples and beer. I've flown thousands of miles to be with him. I want to fix his pain. But I blunder into his grief, asking questions, giving advice.

The first morning arrives cold, dreary. He has already left for work by the time I get up, groggy from jet lag. I stumble into the kitchen to make a cup of coffee, but there's no coffee. Nor is there a coffeepot, or a teakettle, or tea. I settle for an apple and a glass of water.

I rummage through a box of his books, looking for something to read. I find a book by philosopher/theologian James Carse and remember that I sent it to my son when he was in college. Pleased that he kept the book, I flip through the small volume, come upon an essay, "A Shared Silence," in which Carse tells of a lecture he gave at his old school. Carse refines the lecture, polishes it, refines it again, he says. He wants to please Katz, who was his favorite professor.

Carse's mother decides to attend the lecture. She gets a substitute for her fifth-grade class and drives two hours to get there. He watches as she makes her way through the crowd of undergraduates and finds a seat. Carse is embarrassed—his mother has elected to wear a large black hat and white gloves. She basks in pleasure, as if the whole event has been created for her alone.

The lecture goes exceedingly well, Carse says: he looks up frequently, doesn't get lost, finishes on time. A commendable job, he thinks. A few people stop to thank him. He notes that Katz leaves without a word.

Carse takes his mother to a local diner, expecting her to register pride. Had he not earned it? She asks about his children, shares stories about her fifth graders, gives Carse an update on the lives of his brother and sister and their children, tells a lengthy story about her two big smelly dogs. As she gets in the car to leave, she explains that when she is away too long, her dogs poop on the kitchen floor. *So a story about dog poop is more important than my lecture?*

It was years after her death, Carse says, when he came to understand his mother's response. He writes, "The ego, as always, misunderstood the nature of this gift of silence."

I note that on page 159 of the essay my son has underlined the words *not until my mother was long dead*, and has written in the tiniest of letters possible, in pencil, hardly legible, *I don't want my mother to die!* I wonder what fears, what longings triggered that notation, the only one throughout the article. I find a place of silence within.

Over the next few days, my son and I sample the town's restaurants, we eat fat sandwiches and coconut cream pie, with mounds of meringue; we play country music and sing along with the lyrics, in full voice, *the lonely bone's connected to the drinkin' bone*; we cheer as the Golden State Warriors soundly defeat the Pelicans; we go to a movie, a silly comedy, and I laugh so loud that my son shushes me, embarrassed.

After three days, I fly back home. My seatmate wants to tell me about his important job with high tech, about this important trip to India he's on. I smile and turn away, close my eyes. My son's silence is all around me, a shared silence, holding us tighter than ever before.

The Nature of the Beast

WAKING FROM A dream two weeks ago, I had a vision of Tuffy's pawprints. Now I keep flashing on them when I least expect to. I'm in the grocery store, there they are in the cereal aisle, just below the cornflakes. I'm taking a walk in the neighborhood, I see the pawprints appearing on the concrete before me.

I will tell you about Tuffy and the sad thing that happened.

I was a schoolteacher, a high school English teacher in Mobile, Alabama, my first job. Tuffy was my dog. Born on my Uncle Gene's farm in Tennessee, he was a little feist, as we called such a dog in the South, shorthaired and frisky. I chose him from a litter of squirming pups one summer during a visit home. Tuffy was just eight weeks old when I took him, a warm white bundle with a black nose. I put him in a cardboard box lined with old rags in the back seat of my new Mustang, drove down to Charleston to start school in the fall. I didn't know what to call him, decided on Tuffy because he didn't whimper like puppies do

I lived in a renovated Victorian on Government Street, with a stained-glass window from floor to ceiling in the kitchen. When I tried to leave Tuffy alone, he ripped and tore, so I had to leave him outside while I was at work. He was a farm dog, it was just his nature. When I got home each day, he snuggled with me while I marked essays, he cuddled with me as I slept.

These days dogs must be on a leash. But it wasn't that way when I grew up in the South. Dogs slept under the house, ate table scraps, never saw a leash. I went to the coast one weekend, for the beach, left Tuffy on his own. When I came back on Sunday, he ran to my car, delirious with joy, jumped up on the door, dusty from the drive, leaving his little pawprints there.

The next day at school the principal called me to the office—a most unusual occurrence. A veterinarian was on the line. He said Tuffy had been hit by a truck and killed. The driver had called my vet from the number on Tuffy's tag, but nothing could be done. The vet had traced me down by the registration number on the collar. He asked me if I wanted to pick up the body or if he should take care of it. I said he should, I couldn't bear seeing Tuffy dead. When I went out to my car to drive home, I saw little pawprints in the dust on the side of my car, I couldn't stop crying. I left Tuffy's prints there until the rain washed them away.

Why are those pawprints turning up now?

I think about my age, I just turned 67. I think about my sister Amanda, who is dying of cancer. I think about the husband I left behind, foolishly. I think of my son, whose life never quite came together, somehow. I think of all that has happened that I would make happen differently if I could, but I can't. Those pawprints, those tiny roses stamped in the dust of my car, they are the indelible mark, the sure proof that I can't stop loving.

Why I Like Going to the Dentist

A LOT OF PEOPLE hate to go to the dentist. I used to feel that way when I was growing up. I had bad teeth, every time I went to the dentist, I had to have fillings or a tooth pulled. I remember Dr. Torbett saying open up, the shots with a stupendously big needle, the penetrating grinding. No such thing as preventative dentistry then.

Now I rarely have a dental problem, just go to have my teeth cleaned, get a check-up. My dental hygienist is Joanie, a calm and open-hearted woman, friendly without being familiar. She smiles when she greets me, invites me to relax in the big chair, asks if I would like to have a warm blanket, I say yes, she places one around me. She gives me dark glasses, plays soft music, maybe Mozart. I hardly ever rest like this.

As Joanie cleans my teeth, her full breast grazes my arm. She tells me what a good job I have done with my flossing. She tells me about her son, who won an essay prize at school by writing about the mating habits of dragonflies, he will be going to college next year, she will miss him, she says. I don't have to comment, just lie there, open wide.

Joanie doesn't really know me, doesn't know about my bad boss, doesn't know about my failing marriage, doesn't know I have no children. She seems to care in that pleasant, professional way, requiring nothing from me. In the big chair, under the warm blanket, I close my eyes, imagine I could stay there forever. I drift, I float. Maybe this is what death is like—you are held in a warm place, all your worries detach from your brain and waft away. You don't have to do anything, except exist. Or not.

Cover Your Heart, Reach Out Again

I MADE MYSELF go to my aqua exercise class today—but I didn't want to go. I was sad, the kind of sad that has no cause, no meaning, no cure. I eased into the warm water until my shoulders were covered. I felt held, comforted. I sighed, breath deepening.

Raul had been gone for some weeks. Glad to see you back, I said. A casual remark, something you say when words fail. Generally he is the only man in the class. I've noticed the curls in his dark hair, the curves of his broad brown shoulders. I don't really know him, he has kept to himself. But today it was different. How are you? he asked. I just shook my head. How are you today? he asked once again.

I'm just here with my friends, I said.

He said, That's what it's about. He moved toward me, locking his eyes into mine, I was surprised, confused, he reached for my hand, I gave him my hand. He said, My mother died two weeks ago. I opened my arms to him, he held me close for an unconscionably long time, I felt his skin, the warmth of his body, against mine. It didn't matter that the other members of our class were beginning to move in unison to the instructions of the teacher: *Grounding yourself, yes, now pay attention to your core, now open those arms, open them wide, look up.* . . . It didn't matter that I didn't know Raul and he didn't know me.

I said, I'm so sorry.

He said, You don't have to be. She led a good life, a beautiful life, she went out well. He smiled.

That's good, I said. I'm glad.

You see how open I have become, he said.

Yes, I said.

He released me, we moved to our regular places, gave ourselves to the embrace of the water, the movement of our limbs. *Reach out with those arms, pull back, cover your heart. Reach out again.*

The Past Is Not Even Past

The past is never dead. It's not even past.
—*William Faulkner*

MOM WAS A real packrat. Going through her stuff, I ran across a letter, May 1953, well preserved, *Never Sent* scrawled across the top. Something told me not to open it, of course I did:

My Dearest David—
I'm going to be married tomorrow. I didn't want it to be this way, I loved you without reservation—if the truth were known, I still do, here on the eve of my wedding, a year to the day you left. I always knew you would return to the Kibbutz one day, you never misled me. I know your loyalties, I know what your integrity demanded, I knew I would lose you one day.

About Harry—he's a good man, a career army guy who left, now is head of maintenance at the Hilton. I don't understand why, but he adores me, he says, would do anything for me. I want you to know I'll be all right. We're both originally from Modesto, actually have a lot in common—he played on the football team a few years before my time.

You and I decided not to write, we knew that would bring nothing but grief, this will be the only letter I'll ever send you, I don't expect an answer. I want you to know that no man will ever take your place in my heart. I'm remembering a long bus ride one Christmas, going to visit my sister in Chicago. I found a seat next to a woman whose rich dark face was furrowed with age, we talked for hours, she told me about an early love of hers, she said, It was a graveyard kind of love. I asked what she meant, she said one that follows you to the grave. Now I understand.

You will be loved by other women, you will find some-one special—I want that for you, but keep my love in some corner of your heart, let it be something of a ballast against future grief and loss, the kinds of eventualities that come to all of us.

All my love,

Celeste

I stared at the letter, read it again. I recalled Dad's sadness, his distance. He and Mom, totally mismatched, he was a jock, she was a lover of literature, a teacher of English and French. They stayed together, I suppose, for us children. They did us no favor, my sister and I lived under the cloud of their disappointment.

Mom finally left him, he slunk off to a single room in a boardinghouse, where he lived for six years, smoking, watching sports on TV, going to the corner pub to drink, always too much. He was a good-looking man, even as he aged, never lost that dark hair at all, but never kept company with anyone after Mom.

I called one Sunday evening, as usual—no answer. I tried Monday, again Tuesday, then got in touch with his landlady. She found him dead, propped up in bed with a girlie magazine, the coroner said heart attack, he had been gone four days. I wanted a different kind of death for him, a different kind of life, I guess.

Can't blame Mom, she wanted to love him, I guess in her own way she did, but she didn't *like* him, his long silences, the words he chose, the way he putzed around the house, he got the message he was invading her space, I think. And there was his drinking, never drunk, but . . . removed. She was a goddess to him, shining off in the distance, untouchable. He gave her his fidelity, the work of his hands, felt her hunger for what he couldn't give.

Both gone now, so does it stop there? Hardly. Why have I never married? Why did my sister marry a rich guy and dedicate her life to buying stuff? We carry them forward, Harry and Celeste. David, too.

I held the letter to my lips for a long moment. Then dropped it in the trash.

Resistance to Change

Haven't we always known that all of life is change—that in fact, with each breath we change? Nevertheless, accepting the truth of impermanence is profoundly challenging. We become identified with, even defined by, our roles and relationships. Life is ever shifting into new forms though, so clinging to any form, however satisfying, will make us suffer. The ancient adage is true: "Life is a bridge; therefore build no house on it." The spiritual journey is learning not to build houses on the bridge.

Becoming Clear

JUDY AND GEORGIA talk, as all couples do. They try hard to make their wishes and opinions known, each to the other, but they often fail. When Judy fails, she looks at Georgia with squinty eyes and repeats what she just said, only louder. When Georgia fails, she rolls her eyes and says, I just *told* you. Neither thinks to try again, with different words. They each think that the other is simply being difficult.

Interestingly enough, both Judy and Georgia are known as strong, clear communicators in their respective lines of work: Judy is a "creative," producing ads for television, and Georgia reviews films for several notable publications. Both have won plaudits in their fields. Both claim that no one else of their acquaintance commonly misunderstands them.

Judy and Georgia decide to seek help from a therapist. They each present clearly and succinctly. The therapist has no trouble understanding either of them. They have no trouble understanding the therapist. But they continue to have trouble understanding each other. During the therapy session, they fall into their usual pattern.

Judy says, I tell Georgia something and she asks me to clarify. I don't know what she means, *clarify*, because my words are simple and clear. So I say the same thing, thinking that she must not have heard me.

Georgia says, I am asking because I want to understand.

Judy says, What's there to understand?

Georgia says, Never mind. She glances at the therapist, says, See what I mean?

Both Judy and Georgia look at the therapist for confirmation.

The therapist is quiet for a long moment. Then she suggests that they turn, each toward the other, and look into the other's eyes. Judy blinks rapidly, looks at the wall. Georgia looks at the therapist, as if to ask, *why?* clenchs her teeth. Nevertheless, they comply, the therapist is the authority—besides, they are paying a lot of money for this session. Both begin squirming in their seats.

Now what? Judy asks.

What next? Georgia asks.

The therapist says, Just continue to look at your partner's face for about five minutes. I'll tell you when the time is up.

Both Judy and Georgia begin to think that therapy, at least this kind of therapy, is a big waste of time, nevertheless they do as the therapist asks.

As she gazes at Georgia's face, Judy notices she has a tiny mole on the left side of her upper lip, which until this moment she has never seen. She had thought Georgia's eyes were green, but she sees that they are actually hazel. She sees the suggestion of tears hiding beneath Georgia's lower lashes. Georgia notices that Judy's head is smaller than she thought, her nose larger. She notices the deep lines which run from her nose to her chin. She sees what could only be described as fear in Judy's eyes.

When the five minutes is up, the therapist says, Now say what is in your heart to say, each to the other. Judy and Georgia are stunned by this suggestion. They go silent, still. Long seconds pass. The silence becomes vast, filling the room to bursting.

Take your partner's hand, says the therapist.

Judy and Georgia say simultaneously, I don't want to.

Now you are becoming clear, says the therapist.

Blooming

DURING ONE of my depressive modes, I passed by a garden shop and saw a blooming plant, peach-colored and radiant, a begonia the tag said. I'm not really a plant person, never had a garden, never wanted one, but this flower called to me. I needed its sweet beauty. I took it home, found an honored place for it on my front porch, where I sit and read. I checked twice a day, making sure it had the water it needed, pinched off the dead leaves, chucked it under the chin, gave it unabashed admiration. In turn, the plant gave me increasing pleasure.

After two weeks, the blooms fell off. I felt sad, a little betrayed. I took my plant back to the garden shop. I found the young clerk with his trowel and jeans, his face brown from the sun, I held out plant to him. I said, My plant stopped blooming.

He looked at the plant, then looked at me. Seeing the disappointment in my eyes, he smiled kindly. He said, Nobody blooms all the time.

Serial Killer

I HAVE A FEAR of breaking things. I don't mean breaking one of my limbs, no, or dropping a vase, seeing it crash on the floor, or ripping up carpet to replace it. I don't want to break anything that I can't restore to its original form. For example, an egg. What a beautiful shape it is! I like hold it, look at it, but to crack it would be a sacrilege. I am unable to scramble eggs or cook a quiche.

Take deadheading the geraniums on my deck. Once I snap a stem, I can never reattach it. Never mind thinning my carrot crop. I am totally unable to kill any creepy crawly creature—even a flea on my dog or a caterpillar eating my roses. I understand that my actions will be irrevocable. I can kill, I cannot create.

A natural object is flawless, undefiled. Who am I to violate its integrity? To shatter it, like a God? When I break a plant or crush an insect, I sense that I'm breaking something within myself.

I'm not like those Buddhist monks with the red robes I saw on TV who spend months creating a sand picture—a mandala, they call it—then destroy it with one swoop. Everything breaks everything dies, they say. Maybe so. But not by my hand.

To Be Held, and To Hold

MARGETTA was late for the Community for Earth meeting in the basement of the church. She looked for the box lunch she had ordered, found that someone had taken her turkey sandwich. That person, she saw, was Paul, an elderly man with mild dementia. Of course she could not question or confront him. How would it look if she said, Who has my turkey sandwich? causing the other members of the committee to glance around until their eyes fell on the old man. Half the sandwich was gone, anyway.

She frowned. She was forced to take the only remaining sandwich, a soggy mess of cream cheese, avocado, and tomato on whole wheat.

Margetta noticed that some new person had taken the chair she generally chose, the one with the firm seat. She couldn't really interrupt the meeting and say, I need my chair. Besides, it wasn't really *her* chair. She sank down into the only chair left, the red one with the broken springs. She knew that within ten minutes her back would begin to ache. She squirmed, tried to get comfortable.

These incidents caused her to reflect, the voices grew faint. She thought, why do I come to these meetings anyway, if I can't be comfortable? If I can't have the sandwich I ordered?

She surveyed the group. Janine, smiling broadly; Monique, who she knew a short time ago as Fred, slumped in her chair, scribbling notes with the stub of a pencil; Jeff, speaking passionately, as always; Alicia, listening intently, elbows on the worn wooden table. It suddenly occurred to her why she came. She came to sit quietly among these people. She came to be safe, to be a part of things that don't change. She came to hold the earth together, at least this little part of the earth.

Margetta saw Paul's hand shake ever so slightly as he raised the other half of her turkey sandwich to his mouth. She never before noticed how blue his eyes were, how perfect.

Breaking Up Is Hard to Do

SHE LEFT HER front door expecting to find her car in the driveway, but it wasn't there. *It has to be there! I left it there.*

Her car was a Honda, champagne-colored, not a new car, no, but a serviceable car, and she was attached to it the way we become attached to things we touch every day. She liked smelling the leather, touching the cord cover of the steering wheel, liked the happy murmur the engine made when she turned the key—the car always started. She thought, How many things in your life can you say respond so well? She liked the color, champagne, which reminded her of the special bubbly she enjoyed on celebratory occasions. Also her car could be really dusty and nobody would notice.

Where could the car be? She began to think.

She remembered she went to movie at the shopping mall yesterday. *Maybe I left the car at the mall and walked home. Yes, that's it!* But no, it was after dark when she came home, she wouldn't have walked. Another theory arose: it was fall, and the driveway was covered with masses of leaves from the gigantic big leaf maple in front of her home. *Maybe the car is under the leaves. Yes, that's it!* But of course not, no car could hide under a pile of leaves.

The car was there, and then it was not. She had run out of theories. She felt her pulse ratchet up, her fingers trembled as she called the police. An officer came promptly. He didn't seem concerned. Lots of Hondas get stolen, they're easy to start, he said, they're even stealing air bags out of Hondas. I'll make a report, but we may not find it, even if we do, it may be stripped down.

Wow! she said. Wow.

Yeah, it's a real growth industry, stealing Hondas, he said, so easy to start, a kid can do it, may even be kids, taking your car for a joy ride. Happens all the time.

So she called her insurance company. Sorry, the man said. Happens all the time. Portland is the car stealing capital of the world, especially Hondas, they're so easy to start. I'll get you a replacement vehicle. She thought he didn't seem too interested. *I'll never, never get my car back!* She hadn't cried until now.

She got her replacement car—a white Ford. She hated white cars because they reminded her of an ambulance, besides every little speck of dirt shows. *Drives like a tin can,* she thought.

Two months went by. She checked with the police often, her Honda was never found. The insurance company sent her a sum for what they said the car was worth. *They have no idea what that car means to me, its real value.*

She deposited the check, went to several used car dealerships looking for another champagne-colored Honda. She didn't want a metallic blue one, there were a lot of those, she didn't want a black one, which shows even more dirt than a white one. She wanted a champagne-colored Honda with a sun roof, exactly like the one she had.

Not only was it impossible to find another car just like her Honda, but the car dealers were unprincipled people, reprobates. They looked at her body, they talked down to her, they lied with every breath. She liked to think of herself as a positive person, not judgmental toward others. But her experiences with the used car salesmen caused phrases to appear in her thoughts, phrases like *They are such douchebags, the scum of the earth.* She didn't like thinking of another human being this way, it was disrespectful. *But they are all dickheads, that's exactly what they are. Dishonorable snakes in the grass.*

Then her luck changed. Her friend Pat, who knew of her increasingly desperate search for a car, called and said, I think I've found a car for you. Why don't you meet me at Freeman's Used Cars, you can look at it. He said the people at Freeman's were good people, and fair. She had a secret hope that the car might be a Honda, champagne-colored.

As it turns out, the evening she was supposed to see this car, rain fell in thick sheets, she could hardly see, besides she didn't know where she was going. Cars that knew where they were going were whizzing past her, she panicked, took a wrong turn on the expressway, found herself headed in the wrong direction. She put the windshield wipers on extra high, *whap, whap, whap, whap,* still she could barely see in the deluge. She was an anxious person in the best of circumstances, she began fearing for her life, picturing herself lying bloody in a ditch, expiring, all because of the theft of her Honda. She felt anger at the unknown person who had stolen her car, felt a deepening disgust at the used car dealers who had tried to take advantage of her. As the traffic thinned, she realized that she was in a town somewhere several miles south of Portland, she turned around, drove back to Portland. She was heading in the right direction, the rain was letting up.

Her good and true friend was standing in front of Freeman's, holding a black umbrella against the drizzle. Though she was forty-five minutes late, he greeted her like nothing was wrong. He said, Here's your car! He gestured and smiled, as if to introduce her to someone special. She saw the car like an apparition before her. It was not a Honda at all, but a beautiful little Volvo! It was the deepest, richest red she had ever seen, polished and shining. She fell immediately and hopelessly in love. Murmuring in pleasure, she started stroking it all over— the hood and the grille, the doors and the windows, the trunk— proclaiming her affection. She said, I love you, little red car, I love you! I want to marry you! No, really, I do!

Her friend said, Don't you want to take the car for a test drive?

No, she said, I want to buy it right now. Where do I sign? I have the money. And so she dashed off a check, and the car was hers.

Later she considered the incident and wondered if she was fickle—or some might say, even promiscuous. How could she "love" her Honda and then so soon after its loss, love another car? She didn't like to think of herself as disloyal. But as she drove her beautiful red Volvo through the subsequent days and weeks, the Honda became a dim and distant memory. She couldn't recall the color, the way her hands felt on the wheel, the characteristic purr of its engine.

Everything in its time, she thought. *Everything in its time.*

Holding On

I GOT MY CAT Maggie just before Connor and I were about to end our relationship. She was only ten weeks old, a little white ball of fuzz with blue eyes. I took her home from the Humane Society in her cardboard box. Connor brought over a toy he had made for her, just a piece of string tied into a bow at the end. A kind gesture. He tied it to the top of a chair, we watched Maggie bat the bow around. Connor grinned. I smiled at him.

Maggie is getting old, for a cat, she's lived almost the allotted time. That is reality, I tell myself. A reality I don't like. You can always get another cat, people say. But I cannot get another Maggie. I cannot get a cat that was a kitten when I was with Connor. Connor was coldhearted, but I had such passion for him. When we made love, I disappeared. No ego at all.

Weeks after Connor left, his wool sports coat hung in my hall closet. I would go to the closet, bury my face in the coat, remember. It had to end, but I wanted it never to end.

Fly Away

I'M STROLLING down Royal toward Antoine's Annex. What made me think to come to New Orleans in July? It's 102 degrees, and moisture hangs heavy in the air. I guess I just needed to get away—to get back to my roots. The key is to move slowly, one careful foot after the other, avoiding the small craters in the sidewalk in these poorly maintained streets. Easy to fall here.

It's not even noon, and people are already drinking. I pass the dark doorways of the bars that line the streets of the French Quarter. The rancid smell of garbage lingers. I pass the signs hanging down from hole-in-the-wall businesses to lure tourists: Mardi Gras masks; voodoo shops selling curses, blessings, aphrodisiacs; clothing suitable for the heat, thin and breezy.

I come upon a ragtag street band, just forming—three black men and one white guy: trombone, clarinet, bass, and a singer. The trombone player is the lead—he's a skinny fellow in pants that are flowing loose around him. His body is just as loose, as he raises his horn up and down and all around, and the group begins to let go, one by one, with the old gospel tune "We'll Fly Away."

I join in, leaning into the singing—I grew up with this kind of music. People stop to listen: a fleshy woman in skintight snakeskin-pattern pants, cigarette dangling; a bent man whose spine was making great pointed lumps out the back of his black T-shirt. All of us together, singing. I get the feeling that we all wanted to fly away somewhere, somehow, not to the great unknown but to islands of quiet and release, to find the tenderness, the joy awakened in us.

I think of home: the large clean office, the two computers, the damn air conditioning. I hear the chorus one more time, and the music follows me down the street: "Like a bird from prison bars has flown, I'll fly away, I'll fly away."

Denial of Death

We are animal creatures who instinctively reach for life—and at the same time, unlike other animals, we are conscious of death. We are hardly able to imagine that we will one day not exist. If we can accept—not just cognitively but existentially—that we will die, we will live each day we are given with more purpose, more vitality. We will open to dimensions of gratitude and compassion we could not otherwise know.

Death in Springtime

I sauntered into
the neighborhood post office
one shining day—
the first blossoms of the cherry
were pressing spring to come—
and there was no line!
It's these little things
that make the heart sing,
not big stuff like curing cancer.
If that sounds shallow,
hey, I'm just human.
The clerk was handsome as a newborn colt,
From somewhere like the Philippines
Or maybe Korea,
I don't know.

Anyway, I asked,
"What have you got for stamps today—
besides flags and puppies?"
Beaming, he said, "We've got Humphrey Bogart,
we've got Gertrude Stein!"
And he held them up for me to see.
His smile, I kid you not,
filled the space,
He must have loved his job,
and people.
Or maybe he got laid last night,
I don't know.

Sure enough, Bogart was there,
looking rakish as always,
and Gertrude Stein, scowling.

As these two idols
hung there in the air—
that's when it hit me—
the death thing, I mean.
I had a sudden
almost uncontrollable urge
to spit out the truth,
to say, "Why are you smiling,
don't you understand?
You are going to *die*,
and who knows when.
It could be any day,
any day at all,

and this post office
and all the pretty stamps
and all your friends
and your sweetheart
won't matter anymore—
nothing ever again will matter."

But I didn't say that:
Nothing like death
to ruin a spring day.
Instead
I looked at him
with so much love.
"I don't know," I said.
"I think I'll take the Bogart."

Letter to Delta Airlines Customer Service

I AM WRITING to you regarding an incident that occurred during my last flight (Delta #3778) with your airline. It was quite a turbulent flight from Chicago to New York. Not that I mind turbulence—I understand that you cannot control the weather, that sometimes passengers will be bounced about. But on this particular flight, as we were beginning our rocky descent into JFK, the pilot took it upon himself to announce, *In case of a water landing, leave your carry-ons on board.* He did not add, *Everything's going to be all right, folks.* I don't know about the passengers in business class, but those of us in coach, having been carted in like cattle, then jiggled around quite a lot during the flight, fell into a frenzy.

I heard a little Shirley Temple look-alike ask her mother, Are we going to die, Mommy? The businessman next to me began writing a letter to his spouse or lover or whoever. I was moved to pray, but didn't know any prayers except the Serenity Prayer, which I've said so often in my AA support group. I did not want to "accept the things I cannot change," like my imminent death, so the prayer was little comfort.

As it turned out, the plane landed smoothly with little difficulty, a resolution which the pilot no doubt anticipated. We were not in the middle of an electrical storm, no ice was mounting on the wings, no mechanical failures had occurred. No, I realized later, the pilot was giving a standard announcement required by the airline, an announcement which should have been given near the beginning of our flight, as part of the preparatory announcements that no one listens to—not during turbulence at the end of a flight, when everybody on board is terrified and of course listening for some words of reassurance from the pilot. Timing is everything, as they say.

Please pass my message on to those who train pilots, not for flying but for public relations. Many of us who fly, although we understand the principles of aerodynamics, nevertheless do not trust that this big machine we are trapped in, so much heavier than air, can possibly stay up. We don't really believe that oxygen masks are going to pop out and save us if all the air is suddenly sucked out of the plane. We have fantasies about dying after spiraling toward the earth, in a ball of flame. We think if we are unfortunate enough to make a water landing, the lucky ones of us will drown while the others will be attacked by hordes of sharks. These are the thoughts of many of us while we fly, I think I say on good authority. I'm asking that you consider not only the physical well-being but the psychological and emotional health of your passengers. Train your pilots and airline attendants to make us think we are safe, although we know we are not.

Thanking you in advance for considering this issue and taking the corrective steps necessary.

Mammogram

I'M IN THE CLINIC for a mammogram, a follow-up to the one last week labeled "suspicious." I am worried, but not very worried. The letter said most findings were not cancer. On the other hand, my mother died of breast cancer. The technician says, Take your clothes off from the waist up and put on this gown, open in the front. The usual. I go into the cubicle, strip off my clothing. I look down at my breasts, I slide my hand under the left one, soft like a baby's skin. Big luscious flowers, they are. I cover myself with the skimpy cotton gown. I'm ready.

This is going to be painful, she says. We have to get a good picture. You have a lump in your right breast. She pauses, she asks, "Are you on hormones?"

Yes.

For a long time?

Yes.

Her brow darkens, she shakes her head. Or do I imagine this? I'm feeling guilty, stupid.

Let's see if I can feel the lump, she says. She palpates my breast. The flesh gives way to her touch, but she is not sure that she feels anything. She says, "Ummm," frowns.

My heart is picking up its pace. How much chance that this is cancer? I ask. I realize that this is a ridiculous question to ask of a technician, I have to ask it anyway.

She hesitates. I can't answer that, only the doctor can, she says, averting my eyes. But you have been taking hormones a long time, so you are at much greater risk. I think I'm cooked, probably.

When will I know?

Before you leave this place today.

At least I won't have the agony of waiting. She takes the results to the doctor and returns after a few minutes. She says the doctor wants me to have a sonogram.

The sonogram technician comes in, big smile. Teeth even, white. How are you? she says. I don't know how to respond. *I think I might have cancer. How do you suppose I am?* But I don't say this. Her job is hard enough, maybe even boring, taking these pictures all day long. I'm OK, I answer.

She tells me to lie down on a table, she pulls down my gown, exposing my right breast. She puts a glob of cold gel on my breast, just below the nipple, runs a wand in a slow circle over the sticky stuff. I'm looking at the image on a screen. Is that it? I say.

Yes, that's your lump.

It's black, solid, oblong—a dark egg floating in and out of the undulating mass. "Hang on," she says. I have to measure it. Red lines appear above and below, left and right, of my lump. *Clitchit clitchit, clitchit clitchit.* It's there, all right. I see it. My lump.

I don't know how big it is, because I don't know the ratio of the picture to its physical presence in my body. On the screen it looks big.

I have a mass in my body, and it's growing. I shouldn't have taken the hormones. Why did I take them, anyway? Oh, yeah, it was the hot flashes that wouldn't go away. Actually, I know that the increases of breast cancer for those taking hormones is not that great—a few percentage points higher. I tell myself it was not a bad decision to take hormones. But I don't believe myself.

I'm cold, shivering in that gray and white room, waiting for the answer. Thinking of my death. Thought that I would escape dying the way my mother died, probed and poisoned and sliced, apparently not.

I'm considering what I will miss, finding there's not much. Certainly not my job. Wonder if people will miss me, not many, I'm thinking. Maybe my two boys, now getting on with their own lives, their own children. Maybe my best friend Becky. She says I make her laugh. A few people may be sad when I die, but they won't be sad for long, because I'm the one dying, they're not.

The technician returns. She says, Good news—it was just a fluid-filled cyst, nothing more.

I'm okay? I ask, hardly believing her.

Yes, you're good to go, she says.

I am disoriented, have trouble finding the compartment where I left my stuff. Numb, grateful, I dress quickly, stumble into my clothing. I walk out of there, alive.

I'm not going to die. Maybe ever.

Memorial Fidelity

> I believe that everyone in the world wants to
> be with someone else tonight, together in
> the dark, with the sweet warmth of a hip or
> a foot or a bare expanse of shoulder within
> reach. Those of us who have lost that, what-
> ever our age, never lose the longing: just
> look at our faces. If it returns, we seize upon
> it avidly, stunned and altered again.
>
> —*Roger Angell*

JOHN AND I often talk about "What if?" What if one of us
dies first? I am reminded of the story in which a wife says to her
husband, "Dear, if one of us should die first, I think I will go
and live in Paris." It's always someone else, isn't it? John and
I know that it's not someone else—we are in our seventies, we
have seen too many of our friends go. *How long, how long?* No
one knows. But not long.

John and I met over a cup of tea, just a couple of months after his wife Eleanor's death. We fell instantly in love—*oh yes, it does happen*. I saw the transformation in his eyes—he blinked and glanced down, shy like a boy. I am astounded at his need for me, a need which has only grown stronger during the four years we have been together. He is the type of man who needs a woman.

I have told John that if I die first, I would not want him to be alone. That's what I think, not necessarily what I feel. The truth is, I have always been unable to imagine any partner of mine going on to have a relationship with a new woman. *How could he be unfaithful to me?*

What about my own death? How can I be hurt if my partner is with someone new? After all, I'll be dead. Nevertheless, I cannot bear to think of it. If I outlive John, and I think I will, I will open myself to being "stunned and altered again," as when I met him. I want always to allow life to fracture my world and make me new. With as little pain as possible, and no regret.

Dreaming Lola

I SEE HER falling, the little girl with the long dark hair. She cascades, head over heels, twisting, turning, arms out, she's flying, she's floating, slowly passing each floor on her way down, like a colorful manikin in her red tights, yellow top. She makes no sound as she falls. I see her drop to the pavement below, lie still. . . .

Something told me not to let the boys go up to the rooftop garden of our apartment building, some vague intuition of danger. I overrode the warning with logic. It was a pleasant spring day, flowers opening to the sun. My children, ten and eleven, were responsible, sensible. They wanted to show the garden to their new friend Lola. Mom, can we? Can we?

Sure, I answered, and the three raced away. Thirty minutes or so later, I went up to check on them. The first thing I saw as I left the elevator was Lola walking on the ledge of the building, ten stories up. I froze. Lola, you need to come down, I said.

Why? She said, and grinned.

You're not safe there. My hands, arms were shaking.

Oh, really? she said, she put out her arms as though she were balancing on a tightrope. Watch this, she said, continuing around the edge. She had me, and she knew it.

Lola, *please*, I said. You need to come down—now.

Look at this, she said. She balanced on one foot, hopped once, twice.

How about some cookies, I said. Chocolate chip.

Lola looked at me, smiled. She wobbled a bit, jumped down to safety in the garden. I grabbed her, held her tight to my body, tears stinging, Don't you ever, don't you ever, ever, ever, I said.

That happened thirty years ago. I still see Lola in my dreams, falling, I cry out, I wake with a start, I thank whatever gods that be.

Right on Time

EVER SINCE I turned seventy and had my little stroke, I *always* know what time it is. In the middle of the afternoon, I look up from my reading and I think it must be 3:30, and I check the clock and sure enough it is 3:30, or within minutes of that. Sometimes I lie in bed at night, hearing my heart beat out loud—*ker-thump, ker-thump, ker-thump*. It is an encouraging sound, steady and constant. I will generally wake up two or three more times during the night, and hear my heart still at it, and I will look at the clock: 1:30 A.M., yes, I knew that; 4:00 A.M., nailed it again!

I'm afraid it's later than I think.

For Some Time I Thought There Was Time

For some time I thought there was time
and that there would always be time. . . .
                                    —*W.S. Merwin*

I thought there was time
to finish the term paper—
I thought there was time
to pay that bill—
I thought there was time
to get to the play—
I thought there was time
to send the Christmas cards—
I thought there was time
to apply for that job—
I thought there was time
to find my true love—

I thought there was time
to get pregnant—
I thought there was time
to choose another career—
I thought there was time
to take up photography—
I thought there was time
to see the archipelago—
I thought there was time
to thank my father—
I thought there was time
to find the answer—
I thought there was time
to say goodbye.

Not Afraid

THE DOCTOR said in answer to my hapless question, *no one knows how long, everyone is different, I've known those who've gone as long as six months or more,* but the *more* is not years, it's months, I don't believe it, not possible to be me then not me, my Buddhist friends say there is no me anyway, they believe in reincarnation, not all that logical when you consider how many of us there are to reincarnate, I wish I could buy it, but *my* breath is the one to become ragged, *my* heart to stop, *my* body to dress and take to the boneyard or to be eaten by the fire—when the talk about the weather stops, when the talk about the president stops, when the talk about the big pigskin game stops, when the talk turns to those dying or dead, as it eventually does, someone will smile, will say, *I'm not afraid of death*—used to be me, ha, turns out that's a crock.

Loss Brings Anger, Grief, Regret

Our physical selves, so strong and resilient in our youth, decline as we age. It is hard to believe that these legs that have served us so well are becoming reluctant. Eyes, ears, lungs, heart, bones: all weaken with the years. Ideas that once held us firmly in their grasp wear thin, and technology moves us exponentially into a brave new world.

We are surprised by the mounting deaths of family, friends. Saddened, we say unfair, too young. We may become angry—at the one who is gone, at ourselves, at God. We feel that a part of ourselves has been lost, and we grieve, all of us in different ways, and in our own time.

Melissa

WHEN I ARRIVE at Melissa's house, the front door is standing open. I'm a minister, and it is Sunday, so I have just come from the church service. Inside in the hallway, lined up to greet me, are her two grown daughters, Jane and Betsy, her husband Colin. As soon as I see their faces, I know what I will hear. Jane says, Mother is dying. I open my arms wide. I release her, put my arms around Betsy, then Colin, whose frame registers a slight trembling.

Melissa had become my friend after I moved to town a decade ago, the kind of friend you can tell anything to. She was a tall handsome woman with thick dark hair just turning silver at the temples. And she had a most compassionate heart. On Saturday night she had called to wish me well with my Sunday sermon. She told me she had been in bed all day, which was not her way. I had asked her if she wanted me to come. She said no, she was all right, she just needed to rest. She knew I was busy finishing my sermon, she said. Now I realize her call was a good-bye call.

I see Melissa's doctor, standing in the shadows. Melissa is a doctor, too, these women have been friends for years. Will she wake up? I ask.

No, says the doctor, shaking her head, her eyes teary.

Is she in pain? I ask.

No, says the doctor.

I walk down the hall to Melissa's bedroom. I see that she is unconscious, flinging one arm back and forth, then flopping from side to side, as she tries to get comfortable. One afternoon two years ago she had called and said, Come over right now. Never in the long years of our friendship had she ever made such a demand. I invented a story in my head that nothing really serious was going on, all the while suspecting I was lying to myself.

When I arrived, Melissa asked me to come sit with her on the living room sofa. She said, I have colon cancer. I have eight months to live. She paused. Go with me through this, she said.

Of course I will, I said—not knowing if I could. But I did go with her, through surgery, through radiation, through countless quiet moments, listening, laughing about some nonsense, sometimes holding her. She lived for two years. But on this Sunday afternoon I can do nothing more for her. I knew this death was coming. I knew it, but I didn't know it. Now I see her there on the bed, twisting and turning, beyond my reach.

We went shopping, Melissa and I, just a couple of weeks ago. I was looking for a pair of shoes, she came along. Any excuse to be together. I bought a good pair of walking shoes that day, then Melissa told the clerk that she wanted to look for shoes, too. *What was she thinking?* The clerk obliged, brought out a pair of dark red leather shoes, lace-up, comfortable. Real beauties. Melissa tried them on, they fit perfectly. The clerk said, the shoes will last you for twenty years. Melissa paused. Maybe not today, she said.

The scene at the house is absolutely ordinary and predictable. The one dying is ensconced in a bedroom, others coming and going, restless and desolate. Children peeking around the bedroom door, eyes wide, trying to understand what is happening, then scurrying away, or being brought in by parents to say an awkward goodbye. Men running errands, fixing, fetching and carrying, avoiding the sick room. Women organizing food, making phone calls. Women looking after the person who is dying.

The doctor pulls me aside and says, I just gave her morphine, go to her now if you want to say goodbye. I go to the bedroom, no one else is there. Melissa is quiet now, at peace. I take her hand, I stroke her forehead, I tell her I love her. They say hearing is the last of the senses to go, and I want her to know I'm here. Maybe she does, maybe not.

I leave so others may come in and say their goodbyes. Within minutes Melissa is gone. There are arrangements to make, tasks for the living, people scurry away. I climb into bed with Melissa, my body down the length of her body. I know coldness will come to her flesh soon, now I can feel the warmth still lingering there. I ask myself why I am reluctant to leave. There is no answer, just my body insisting it wants to be next to her body.

Everyone leaves the house except the daughters and the husband. We are waiting for the hearse. They will be bringing a body bag for Melissa. Two stout men from the funeral home will put her in that bag, take her away. I've seen the process too often, I do not want to see it this time. Nor do I want her daughters to have this as a last memory, so I take them into the living room. I let Colin see her out. He leaves her wedding ring on, he wants it to be cremated along with her.

The hall clock ticks. Long minutes pass. I hear the door slam, at last. The engine revs up, the hearse pulls out of the drive.

The house has an eerie emptiness about it, no one is speaking, we are dull, flattened with loss. I haven't eaten since early morning, I know part of my weakness is from lack of food. I take my leave, drive to the Cadillac Café on Broadway, near my house. It is a small and crowded restaurant, run by two gay men. They know me here, the guys and the waitstaff. It is good to be known just now, to be comforted by the sound of familiar voices and faces. I say nothing about Melissa, about her death, but they read in my face some kind of devastation. *Can we get you anything, Darlin'?* Their little kindnesses touch me deeply.

I hear the people around me talking about their petty issues, their gossip. I hear their laughter. It all seems so beside the point. I am suddenly famished. I order poached eggs and big, thick slices of bacon and two blueberry pancakes, which I slather with butter and maple syrup, and coffee and orange juice. Enough for two people. I eat in the midst of the restaurant buzz, the hum of community. I am in my own interior space. I eat and eat and eat. I eat to live. I leave a tip twice as big as usual.

I walk out into the world again.

The Way of All Flesh

Eventually, all things merge into one, and a river runs through it.

—*Norman Maclean*

HAVEN'T SEEN MY high school classmates in fifty years, haven't been back to that little town in Georgia except for my daddy's funeral seventeen years ago. I'll wow everybody, surprise them. The motherless girl with the alcoholic father has made good, has lots of books to her name, a solid marriage. They'll see the clothes, the haircut, the vintage diamond on my finger.

Sarah greets me as I walk down her driveway to the party. She says, Seven of us are gone, two suicides, says it right off, without blinking an eye. Doesn't know she will be next, with a heart attack the following fall. Guess that's why I never received the photos.

Susan is there, the beauty queen, one breast gone, two husbands gone, the first in a car crash, the second, a good ole boy with money she divorced after he hit her too often. She shows me a picture of her granddaughter, a déjà vu moment—looks exactly like Susan looked in high school. Same stunning smile, same brown curls. Like we were then, our lives stretching out before us.

I spot Ann, star guard on our basketball team. I could rebound but couldn't dribble, Ann would get the ball down the court. She can't rise because of her recent stroke. I spent the night once at her home in the country: the outhouse, the cow, her thin, soft-spoken mother with skin like cream, the sweet butter she churned, spread thick on molasses cookies. The service on Sunday at the little country church, where thirty worshipers belted out hymns that sustained them. Betty can still talk, so we do.

Ray, the quarterback of our "Iron Men," head thrown back, still looks handsome and commanding, if a bit thicker at the waist. He has a car dealership, he says. Actually a couple of them, used and new. Eight grandchildren. We all thought he would make something of himself, apparently he did.

Robert, one of our two drum majors, has become a pediatrician, later a "board certified psychiatrist," because as he says, Sometimes you just need to understand things. His wife Emma was not there, she was dying of some wasting disease whose name I can't remember. Robert reminds me that we used to compete for grades, I never thought that.

The other drum major, Eileen, introduces me to her West Point husband, a lanky, gracious man who had done his time in Vietnam, left when he could no longer stomach our presence there. She once sent me a Christmas card with a tank on the front. Now they are touring the country in their bus-size RV for a year, she says, laughs at its size. Eileen was the DA's daughter, an only child, the only one in our class who had both piano and art lessons. She has written a self-help book about happiness, for a while had a regular TV show of her own, she says.

Denny has a pudgy round face, not the thin freckled one I remember, I don't know him at first. I ask about his older brother Sam, he glances away, reminds me that Sam killed himself years ago. Oh, yes, I remember now, I say, then change the subject.

Jimmy Jack, another of the Iron Men, is retired from his position as principal of the private school out by Lake Tobias, the one where the whites went after integration came. He has put on a lot of weight, I recognize him by the jut jaw that always made him look tough. He was gentle, except on the field. The high school is all black now, except for a few poor whites, he says, and in disrepair, the broken windows, the football field uncared for, so sad. He shakes his head, takes another chicken salad sandwich. Even the swimming pool, the Olympic-size one up by the hospital, has a crack up the middle, had been dry for years, he says. It's where we all went swimming every day in the summer, Daddy always said the blacks had their own pool, but I didn't believe it. Now nobody has a pool.

Kenneth is still there in our little home town, selling sporting goods. A steady kind of guy. I ask him, Who were they, the suicides? He grows quiet, then speaks, hardly above a whisper. One was David, he says. I flash on the shy sweet boy with dark-rimmed glasses and pale skin, the one I had a crush on in the sixth grade—he never knew. Another was Allen, he had polio

77

and crutches, red hair and freckles, ever cheerful, he lurched along while others walked and ran.

The banquet that night was supposed to be a celebration. It starts with photos of us when we were in high school, we laugh and wipe our eyes, remember our small triumphs, our misdeeds. Then people start telling stories about the dead classmates, the party turns into a wake, this goes on for three and a half hours, the restaurant has to close. The men shake hands, the women hug the ones nearby, we all go our separate ways. The rest of the program never happens.

I leave the evening sober, stunned. I see it all spread out before me: the terrible illnesses that surprise, the mistakes, the betrayals, the chances we take, the fears that drive us, the loss— the hopes washed thin with living. The absolute fall to the earth, in the end.

The Fly God

I NOTICED the fly one chilly day in early spring. I was in the stripped-down duplex I was rehabbing, waiting for the contractor to show up. Ignoring the clear signals that summer had not as yet arrived, I stood shivering in my T-shirt and shorts, glimpsed a shaft of gold streaming through the dining room window, walked over to stretch and warm myself—that's when I saw him: a monster housefly, easily the largest I have ever seen. Must have been a fly granddaddy, a fly king, maybe a fly god. But for his color and tepid manner, he could have been mistaken for a bee.

The fly was crawling around the edges of one of the panes, trying to follow the light out. He knew there was another world outside the glass, a world of flowers, budding trees, best yet, fresh dog shit. He wanted to be there, not trapped inside. He moved slowly, almost in resignation, one tiny black leg after the next. He did not give up. When he traversed the perimeter of one pane, he stumbled over to the next, continued doggedly on, circling round the edge. I wanted to open the window, granting him his freedom, the windows had been painted shut. I considered capturing him in a paper bag, releasing him to forage for garbage or check out the dead squirrel in the street, but I didn't have a paper bag, the house was empty. There was no escape.

Does escape really matter though? Houseflies live only two to four weeks, so in the scheme of things, he had maybe a day to live. A dreary forecast! Is a day worth all this excruciating effort? This aging, arthritic fly should probably fold his wings, Zen-like, and die with grace.

I suppose, though, he's alive until he's dead. He will endlessly round the perimeter of his cage, painfully pushing the edge of darkness, looking for the light, hoping in vain for a way out.

The Day My Books Fell

CONSTRUCTION is going on outside my condo window while I am trying to write an essay, "The Philosophy of Meaning: A Retrospective" for *Journal Philosophique*. Big yellow trucks, giant Caterpillars, every day except Sundays. I close the windows, still the sound invades. *Thump, thump, thump, beep, beep, beep*, loud and insistent.

I notice that my computer keys are trembling as I touch them, as though the letters are trying to escape. Then I realize that my desk is vibrating, *thump, thump, thump*. Shortly my whole study feels unstable, the books rise from the shelves, first one, then three, then many, hitting the floor. Kierkegaard comes down, Dostoevsky, Sartre. Tillich falls, and Rilke. *Is there an earthquake?* I run to the window, the scene outside is calm, only the river shining in the sun, the heavy equipment still for the noon hour, people strolling by. That's when I think to put my hand on the big artery in my neck. I hear the sound there, *thump, thump, thump*, feel the vibration. I understand at once: my heart is trembling, all my books are coming down.

Urban Lesson

I'M OLD. Not old old, just old. I recently had a fall and injured my hip, I'm having to use a cane, which I hate. Makes me feel old old. I had just left my health club, or I think they call it, fitness club, where I did my warm pool exercise with Janie, my physical therapist. Walking back to my condo, I came upon a pod of children from the neighborhood Montessori School, seated on the sidewalk. They were with their teachers, though these two hardly looked old enough to teach anyone.

The kids were taking up the whole sidewalk, having some kind of urban lesson I guess. When I got closer, I thought they would move, like anyone would, to let an older person by, they didn't. I stopped, stone still, I waited. They didn't even notice I was there. I raised my cane in the air, I said, Wake up! Wake up, look around you! You're not the only ones in this world. Just because you're young, you don't get to take up the whole sidewalk.

The children—boys in their short pants, girls in their flounces—stopped like little statues, stared. The teachers got all wide-eyed, herded them closer. I walked slowly by them, looking straight ahead. Just because you are *cute*! I said, as I passed through.

What We Say When There's Nothing Left to Say

SEVERAL MONTHS ago my old friend Jane called, lung cancer, metastasized to the brain now. I sent her cards, little gifts, an amaryllis at Christmas, trying somehow to reach her—to save her, I suppose.

Jane and I were in a writing group together for eight years while we were raising our children in Kentucky. She knows about my depression, my flagrant misjudgments of men. She knows about the oppressive blue wall-to-wall carpet that covered the entryway and living room of my Victorian home. She was there when I left my marriage, ripped up my oppressive blue wall-to-wall carpet, turned the wooden floor of my Victorian into a disco for parties. She listened as I blurted out the story of my father's murder. She was there when I went off to a new life in California.

I was with her when she cut her waist-length raven hair into a bob. I heard her stories about the lawyer husband she loved, who didn't know how to love her. I was there when she began publishing her poems in literary journals, when she began teaching at the University of Kentucky. Later she became the Poet Laureate of Kentucky. All her life she has lived in a farmhouse in Versailles (pronounced ver-sales), Kentucky, that has been her family home for generations.

I had sent Jane my new book, a memoir that included those days in Kentucky when we were young, could still imagine new lives, new choices. She has read my book, wants to talk. I ask her how she's doing, which seems as I say it a ridiculous question. She makes some brief, vague answer. We talk about our writing group, the circle of women figuring out our lives, the lives that lay so abundantly before us. She says, My daughter (the one she calls Tater) is pregnant for the first time at thirty-nine, it's a girl. I want to see that baby. She hesitates. She says, completely without self-pity, but with surprise, I always thought I would be an old woman. When do we understand we are not immortal? she asked.

She wants to know what I'm writing these days, I tell her I'm obsessed with death, writing about nothing else, mostly funny stuff.

Yes, death is pretty funny, she says, not a trace of irony.

It's my only way in, I say. I can't imagine not existing. But Jane, art lasts. Poems last, books last, our work remains. She does not comment.

Jane's voice is getting weaker, she needs to close out the conversation. She says, I'll let you get back to your life now. I want to give her something, something to keep her safe, some magic to make her live. Those years we had together rest between us. I say what you say when there is nothing left to say: I love you, Jane. She says, I love you, Marilyn. It's what we are allowed. It seems enough.

Thinking of the Key,
Each Confirms a Prison

title from T. S. Eliot, "The Wasteland"

I TURN THE TAP, no water. Strange—no warning, nothing. Go downstairs to Stephanie's apartment, door standing halfway open. I call out, Stephanie? Call again, louder, Stephanie? No answer. Open the door wider, notice on wall faded spot where a cuckoo clocked used to be. Enter the apartment gingerly, look around. Empty, light streaming into the bare space, balls of dust scurrying across the floor, floating in the sun. I see the super in black T-shirt with arms torn off, hunched over the kitchen counter texting. I ask, Where's Stephanie?

Moved, he says, not glancing up.

Moved? I just talked to Stephanie last weekend, I didn't hear anything about moving. Where'd they go?

I have no idea, he says. Absolutely no idea. Continues texting.

Why is the water off?

Glances up, irritated. Don't know. Trying to figure that out, lady. Just trying to figure out stuff.

Visit to Father at the State Hospital

Face gray, eyes stare
blank sockets into space,
fingers still, stiff
on thin thighs, resting, waiting out this scene.
Dead to me already,
you draw slow breath, steady like our old kitchen clock.

Is this my father,
the one whose hand pulled down mountains,
whose body wrote the boundaries of love?

Red-soaked eyes,
mouth innocent like a child's, sweet with want.
You consumed us all—five wives, two daughters—
pulled us to your need
like a starving dog goes growling to the bone.

It's way past time, old man:
Redemption sits like an over-priced bauble in a pawn shop,
glitter gone, dust crusts,
you're determined to decay.

And yet if I could choose,
I would not have you go this way.
I want to remember you diving from the high board,
falling clean and clear, cutting through the water,
coming up triumphant from the depths,
throwing the hair back out of your eyes,
turning your head to heaven.

I cannot choose—
but let it be said, my father,
for those who love you less than I:
if I could choose,
I would not have you go this way.

Those Who Hold Us,
Then and Now

Parents, grandparents, extended family, true friends, teachers—these are the people who nurture us, heal us, love us into being. They allow us to see our own worth; from them we take the values that sustain us. We find their love is remarkably persistent, carrying us into our uncertain future, bringing healing and redemption to all our days.

The Doll

A DOLL watches over me as I write. She is a strawberry blonde, hair piled on her head, tendrils framing her face. Her dark eyes are filled with wonder, mouth slightly open, as if she might speak of some delight. Her dress is peach-colored silk, trimmed with hand-crocheted lace. Oh, and she's pregnant, roundness puffing out the soft tucks of her dress.

I'll tell you how she came to live with me. Elizabeth, an elderly friend of some means, elegant and self-possessed, confessed to me that she felt herself to be too serious. She spent her days using her wealth and influence to address the ills of our community; I was a parish minister, unpartnered, too busy to even consider dating. Neither one of us, we decided, had much imagination for fun. We resolved to change that. Elizabeth and I made a pact: each month we would alternate in inviting the other to some activity that was frivolous.

And so we began. She invited me to see the newborn baby elephant at the zoo. The following month I invited her to a dollmaker's shop—not a shop of your run-of-the mill cherubs that coo and cry, cheap factory-made playthings to be dismembered by careless children or thrown under the bed and forgotten, but rather a shop of custom-made creations by the shop owner and other noted doll makers. These dolls were works of art.

We wandered aimlessly through the crowded shop—so many beauties! Each had its own personality, its own predilections. There were realistic infants that invited holding; a sweet baby girl in a full-length white lace christening dress; a dark brown boy doll named Michael, standing out amidst all the whiteness; an Emily Dickinson doll, with a book in her hand; a winter doll in a velvet coat trimmed in white fur and a matching hat; a prim prairie school teacher doll in unadorned clothing—each a unique vision of the dollmaker, each waiting for the special owner who would ask the doll to fill some unaccounted for empty place in the heart.

Then I saw her—"Samantha: Lady in Waiting," as she was named. I was transfixed. The craftsmanship, the beauty of form and color! Still, the strength of my covetousness surprised me. Her impeccable dress, her care of person, were not self-conscious, but rather born of a confidence that she was worthy, a confidence I had never owned myself. She needed nothing, was whole, complete—and all she was, was in service to the new life within. I wanted that doll. I glanced at the price tag: $400. No way would I ever think of buying her.

The following December I was all set to move into a new home, a Craftsman in a historic district, an area of giant big-leaf maples forming a canopy over wide streets. But the move was not to be—an ice storm of unusual ferocity struck in the night, downing tree limbs and electrical wires. Residents were warned to stay off the streets—of course, the moving van could not get through. So I was left with two empty houses, one I had just vacated and the other cold and empty, waiting to be filled. I was forced to seek shelter with a friend. On the way, fearing damage, I drove by my new home. The streets were covered with black ice, I inched along, safe because no one else was attempting these treacherous streets.

When I reached my house, I tapped the brakes oh so gently to stop, then gingerly made my way up the walk, then up the six slippery steps to the front porch. There I discovered a nondescript cardboard box. *What could this be, who had left it?* I opened the box, peered through tissue paper. Samantha stared up at me, as if to say, "Well here I am, home at last." No note was attached, none needed. But how had Elizabeth driven the five miles to my home? She would have had to cross an ice-coated bridge, would have had to risk downed live wires, limbs across streets, would have had to walk up the treacherous stairs of my home carrying a rather large box. All this she did. In her eighties, and frail, this she did.

Elizabeth did not know my story, it was too close to confess. But somehow she knew.

I remember the day we left.

We were living in Cincinnati, in a two-story white house across the street from Holy Name School. Big Papa and Uncle Gene drove up to our house one day in July. Mother wasn't home. Daddy spread a sheet on the floor, pulled out drawers, dumped our clothes inside. He tied the sheet up, threw it in the back end of Big Papa's black Studebaker.

I asked my father, Can I take my bride doll? No, Daddy said, we can just take the clothes.

My little brother and sister and I crowded into the car, Uncle Gene drove us fast, out of Cincinnati, into the countryside, across the river on a small railroad bridge with no rails, on across the state line to Kentucky, on towards Louisiana. I was nine years old. I didn't see my mother again until I graduated from college.

So the circle has come round.

When I hear the voice of authority telling me that my work is shallow, a woman's babbling, Samantha reminds me to claim my own authority.

When I become convinced that my writing is a waste of time, she tells me that my writing is a sacred calling, not to be dismissed.

When there's something I definitely don't want to write about, she tells me that's where the energy is, to follow it when I'm ready.

When I lack confidence, believing that all I have to say has been said before, she tells me that no one has written what only I can write. Just begin, she says.

When I reach for words and draw a blank, Samantha says, Elizabeth died last year, write about her. Write about me.

Unimportant Things I Remember

CERTAIN MEMORIES jump into my head for no good reason, I mean memories that are not significant, nothing like that first kiss or a death in the family. I'm cutting the grass or taking a walk, there they are, crowding my brain. They keep returning, as if they have an honored place.

I was in the fifth grade, rehearsing for a Christmas concert at my elementary school. The fifth grade teacher, Mrs. Linton, a cold stick of a woman, walked past the choir members, her hand curved round her ear, listening for quality control. She bent over me, cocked her head and listened, then turned to the music teacher, said, You're not going to let *her* sing, are you? The music teacher shook her head no.

The thing is, my next door neighbor, Mamie, had already made me a costume—only a white square with a red tie in front, but it was good of her to make it, my mother had died a year ago, couldn't make one for me. I wasn't much of a singer, I guess, but it was only a Christmas program in our little school, how good do you have to be to sing in a children's Christmas program?

It's not as though I was hurt, I mean permanently, by being excluded, I was a clever girl and pleased my teachers all through school, I won awards in college and graduate school, made Phi Beta Kappa, for years I've been a tenured college professor in one of our better universities. I have not been lucky in love. Some people have called me "self-contained," I guess they think I don't need anyone.

I do, I do.

But no relationship sticks, somehow.

It's a cold Friday night in December, and I've been grading exams. Not what I want to do on a Friday night, but the papers are there for me. Getting up to make a cup of tea, I hear faint voices of carolers. Enter white squares, red bows, children's voices, "Away in a Manger," Mamie's ruddy round cheeks and gray eyes, Mamie kissing away my tears, It's all right, it doesn't matter, sweetheart. It doesn't matter at all.

How Love Stays

AN OLD FRIEND came for a visit. Not exactly an old friend—Fred was a man I might have married. We met at Ben Franklin High School in New Orleans, a public school for gifted students, where he taught math, me English. We hadn't seen each other for years, then one summer he had occasion to attend a conference in Portland, Oregon, where I had made my home. We found ourselves on a summer night sitting in wicker rockers on my broad front porch at dusk, drinking glasses of cool white wine, reminiscing. Our hair had grown gray, the possibilities of youth had long been left behind. I had married, then divorced over thirty years ago, had two grown children and one grandchild. He had never married, had never even had a partner. Though time had brought change, as it will, Fred seemed much the same—still strikingly handsome in that tall blond Nordic way and a bit overbearing. As for me, I was still terminally serious, and a good listener.

The position in New Orleans was my very first job. I had grown up in a small town in North Louisiana, attending a Southern Baptist church three times a week, and I had never been to the big city, not even Shreveport, miles away. I didn't drink, didn't believe in premarital sex, so New Orleans was in many ways an uncomfortable fit for me. Fred, on the other hand, was a sophisticate. The son of wealthy rice farmers, he lived in the French Quarter in a three-story house filled with antiques and art. He taught high school not because he needed money but because he loved teaching, loved his senior math students. He introduced me to beignets and coffee with chicory, to antiques, to opera, to Mardi Gras, to the history and architecture of the French Quarter. We became friends—not close, though, for Fred never let anyone too near. He had many clever and worldly acquaintances, no real friends. His true companion was Skipper, a brown and white mongrel who, unlike the human species, was incapable of betrayal.

Then one evening everything changed. Fred and I decided to drop into a club for drink—yes, I had decided to have a drink now and then, and that evening I had more than one—as we sat close in a curved lounge chair in that darkened space, I turned to Fred, kissed him full on the mouth. We were both surprised. He blinked, stars flashed. He seemed pleased, also profoundly disturbed. He shrank back, looked away, shy, like a schoolboy.

Nothing more was said, but the next week at school, he pulled me aside, said he wanted to talk. He confessed that he loved me. Then he said that he was gay. He wanted to be with me, he said—he was going to consult a psychiatrist to see if he could change.

Fred and I met again, he reported what the doctor had told him: he could waste a lot of time and money, but probably would never be successful changing who he was. Fred said he regretted that we could never be more than friends. I accepted that, our friendship became genuinely close, but never romantic. Six years later I married, moved with my husband to Liverpool, England, where he had a surgery residency. Over the years Fred and I stayed in touch through Christmas cards, the occasional phone call, a visit or two I made to New Orleans.

That hot summer night on my front porch, to the tune of crickets *chirping, chirping*, we caught up with our lives. He told me that since retiring from teaching, he had traveled widely, in particular to hear organ concerts. He was in Portland to hear a major concert. He began musing about the past, considering what might've been. He told me that since Skipper died, he had been very lonely, that travel was losing its allure. He said he wished he had children. He wondered what his life would have been like had he been able to marry me and have a family. Sadly, in his era, he couldn't imagine being married and having children.

My life had gone in such a different direction—he was an atheist, an aesthete, I was a parish minister, trying to help myself and others find God. He was awash in money, I was financially comfortable, wondering if I was too comfortable for a supposed woman of the cloth. Yet for all our differences, I loved the man, loved his intelligence, his arrogance, his anger at civic incompetence, his pride in New Orleans, his understanding that the past never disappears, haunts us all in various ways.

But all I could do these many years later was to pour a little more pinot grigio, listen, touch his hand, let him read in my eyes that I still loved him, insofar as we could love. I had to let him go that evening, I have not seen him since.

When Hurricane Katrina came, I called. He was disheartened, was moving to Houston, he said. Fred in Texas? I can't imagine him not wandering in dusty antique shops; not in his house on Decatur, jampacked with collections of fine china and silver and blue dishes and portraits of nude men; not without Skipper, tongue hanging out, trotting behind; not badgering his students to prepare them for Ivy League schools. I can't imagine him not tall and blonde and heroic, in his own way, alone because he could find no way to be close to another.

How is it that love persists, so stubbornly, through the years, holding fast somehow, refusing all logic and distance and difference. How does it go, and at the same time, stay?

The Nightgown

LAST NIGHT I put on a gown my mother used to wear, soft white cotton, tiny pink rosebuds lining the neck, wide skirt reaching to the floor. I remember Mother like a vision in her flowing white gown. From time to time, I take it out of its box, put it on. It makes me feel beautiful and safe.

The truth is I am not beautiful, not even the least bit pretty. I was gifted with a sharp chin and an equally sharp nose, all from my paternal grandfather. These features made him look clever and serious, like the banker he was, but for a woman, not so good.

And feeling safe? I breathe in fear and breathe out fear, fear wakes me each morning, hovers round me all day, I stay busy to distract myself. Losing Mother may have brought the fear, I don't know. She died in a pedestrian accident on my second birthday, she picked up a cake for my party, on the way home was hit by a truck. You know they say, I could get hit by a MACK truck—well, she was actually hit by a MACK truck. Oddly enough, the cake wasn't damaged.

I was not a neglected child. My father and I moved in with his parents, and my grandmother (I called her Monnie) took over the mother role. She did quite a commendable job, especially considering her age. It wasn't like having a mother, Monnie didn't have the energy she needed for a small child, but she did her best, I have to hand it to her. I continued to have birthday parties, warm dinners every night, a swing to swing in, an apple tree to climb. Monnie sat in her big easy chair and read the Bible out loud every day: "Bless the Lord, O my soul, all that is within me, bless His holy name." She prayed "The Lord's Prayer" with me each night before sleep. I owe her a lot.

Last night was the twentieth anniversary of Mother's death. I took the gown out of the tissue, pulled it over my head. It ripped down one of the side seams, I twisted my body to look, the other side ripped, I raised my arm, the sleeve tore, everywhere I touched it, it came open, I was standing there in shreds of cloth.

I stepped out of the remains, dropped the fabric to the floor. I stood in front of my full-length mirror. My skin was gleaming, lovely, my breasts, full and giving, my sweet, round tummy, my private parts with thick, dark hair. I knew the time had come. There was something I must do, must become. I felt ready.

Am I afraid? I don't know. It doesn't matter.

How I Got Saved

I am the King James Version
I am the old rugged cross
I am the Confederate soldier on the courthouse
  lawn
I am butter and honey on biscuits
I am the warm egg in the nest
I am Stars and Stripes forever in the marching band
I am the ancient Singer sewing machine with the
  foot pedal
I am the wooden plow my grandfather pushed as he
  tilled the garden
I am peaches going hot into the jar
I am wild plums made into jam, chinkapins shaken
  from the tree
I am the fiery preacher at the revival, saving souls
I am the handsome football coach run out of town
  by an angry husband

I am the laughter of my aunts in the kitchen,
    making cornbread dressing at Christmas
I am the town library decorated with the heads of
    African animals
I am Gunsmoke and Dragnet and the Hit Parade
I am Dreaming of a White Christmas in a town that
    never saw snow
I am Love Me Tender on a 78
I am the neighbor who regularly chased her older
    son out of the house with a broom
I am the red-headed doctor who came to my home,
    took my temperature, comforted me
I am my good dog Rusty, who got run over
I am the prayer circle of teens Sunday night after
    church, singing Kumbaya
I am Julius Caesar, The Rime of the Ancient
    Mariner, Great Expectations
I am mayonnaise and tomato sandwiches in the
    summer
I am Easter with white gloves
I am Miss Altalene, helping me choose fabric at
    White's Dry Goods
I am my father's clothes, black with oil and gritty
    with sand, when he came home from the rig
I am the sign BREAD MILK WORMS at the country
    store that sold us bait
I am the silver water tower, shining in the sun
I am the singing coming from the black church,
    where we teens parked and listened

I am the baptismal water that took me under, the
    preacher's arms that held me
I am the cornbread sizzling in the iron skillet
I am the baby rabbits, born on Easter, in our
    backyard coop
I am the big blue-green Olds, in which I learned to
    drive
I am the Sunday Shreveport *Times*, which told me
    about a world outside my town

The Wind Under My Wings

AS A MINISTER, I love all my congregants—that is to say, I wish mightily for the health of their bodies and for the salvation of their eternal souls. But some congregants I like more than others. And some few, I fall in love with. Not in the carnal sense, but in the way we are mysteriously drawn to certain people. Some deadness in us becomes alive again in their presence. Our disappointment in ourselves is forgotten, and we begin to find ourselves quite likable again, the way we were before we learned we were imperfect creatures. That's how it was for me with Tom.

Tom was a pilot, and more than anything loved to fly. He was rakishly good-looking: blond hair, mustache, sunglasses, always. The precision of piloting gave way to an easy playfulness and charm when he was out of the cockpit. When I was around Tom, I always felt sexy and fun, even though I am not sexy and fun. I am an overly serious female minister, unmarried. I'm an outsider, a helper. People never invite me to parties, they come to me when their marriage is falling apart or when their parent dies. Being with Tom felt like being at a party, at a party where I belonged.

Then the unthinkable happened, as it predictably does in this world: Tom was diagnosed with ALS. He stopped flying professionally, then stopped flying altogether. At first his limbs were not much affected—the disease attacked his vocal cords, his speech became labored. We went out to eat, the waiter refused to look at him. I chatted with him after church most Sundays. When words became difficult, he used a computer to communicate. Still handsome, still charming, through it all. He asked me to come to his home so that we could talk about his memorial service.

I know about death. As a parish minister, I have learned to behave as a professional. But I was undone by Tom. As I began asking him what he wanted for readings, for music, tears began slipping out of my eyes, they wouldn't stop. Tom tapped the keys and his machine spoke: *Death happens*, it said. I paused for a moment, taking that in. Yes, death happens, I said, but the only thing wrong with that is that you miss people you love. Tom tapped out another message: *Attachment—get over it.*

I'm so not over it.

Later in the conversation I asked Tom if he had a favorite animal, one that was a spirit source for him. He smiled his crooked smile, then tapped out, *The eagle*. Of course! The eagle is sacred to many Indigenous cultures. The legend of the eagle goes like this: as an eagle grows old, his wings become heavy, his eyes covered with mist. He goes in search of a fountain. He flies up to heaven, up to the sun, where he singes his wings, heals the fog in his eyes in the warm rays of the sun. He then plunges downward to the fountain where he dips himself three times, is renewed with splendid new plumage, perfect vision.

What about life after death? I asked Tom.

He tapped again: *There is no choice—we have more work to do.*

Tom took me flying once, in his two-seater. The sound of the engine, the bumpy climb through the summer air, the tilting of the wings back and forth as we rose—all this frightened me. But when we began gliding over houses below, like toys, over the ribbon of the river, over the bridges with tiny cars creeping along, over the church, even, where the steeple appeared when the clouds cleared, when we were up there with the wind and the sun, I knew that all I saw beneath me was perfect, and in place, I was perfect and in place, so was Tom.

Tom died in his sleep a few weeks later, his little white Yorkie cuddled in one arm. The church was packed. The choir sang, for Tom had been a longtime member, always wearing his sunglasses during the anthem. He told the choir director some of the pieces made him tear up.

I did not cry when I spoke at the service, as I thought I might. I was clear and strong. Well, I always was, around Tom.

The Unguarded Face of Love

My Dear, Dear Daughter—

I'm sending this message by post, rather than our usual emails. Some sentiments deserve pen and paper.

So Michelle has left—for good. I know you are heartbroken. She was your first love, and you never wanted anyone else. I'm so sorry.

I'm remembering those days, those years, of crushing pain after your dad died. My world fell apart. It was surreal. For weeks I couldn't accept that he was gone—how could a man so adept in the wilderness go off snowshoeing and never return? I kept thinking he would come through the front door, smiling, stomping in his big brown boots, shaking the snow off his jacket. It was so hard, never finding the body, never knowing what his last moments were like, maybe lying injured, knowing he was facing death.

I had to find a reason to go on. You and Julie were small, I tried to hide my grief, to protect you. But I know you must remember my red eyes, the tears that slipped out at awkward times, like when I was trying to read you a story at bedtime—and of course at Christmas, the day your dad left for what we thought was a brief foray from our cabin on Mt. Hood. The Christmas tree was up, with its twinkling lights, the familiar ornaments we had collected through the years from family and friends, the colorful wrapping paper, ribbons, still strewn on the floor.

I guess what I'm trying to say, my darling, is that people are always leaving—there's no helping that. They move away, seeking new frontiers (who would have guessed that your sister would find love in the Netherlands and settle there?). People die, sometimes when you least expect it. And sometimes people leave because, for whatever reason, they feel they must.

As much as you love Michelle, or anyone, for that matter, you must find meaning in your life that transcends any one relationship. Why, my lovely daughter, were you created? That's the big question looming over all our fragile lives. Eventually, pain and loss sweep through, turn our expectations upside down. We are pushed deeper, we are forced to search out the answers to the most profound of questions.

My own search led me to cultivate strengths I never even knew I had—and ultimately led me home. I mean, led me to the ground that was stable under my feet—in my case, led me to creativity and to kindness: I paint, I teach, I care. I care for you and Julie and my grandchildren, but also for many others—Annie, our neighbor, who had a fall recently and is not doing well; the servers at the corner restaurant, I know these young people all by name, I am watchful of them; and of course, I care deeply for my students. All artists carry so much doubt about themselves and their work—how could we not? We aspire to an ideal we can never fully reach. I have realized that the blessing comes in the striving.

I know you and Julie don't want to talk about it, but there will come a time when I myself will be leaving you. Age is catching up with me, I can't stand in front of my easel for hours the way I used to.

I'm not planning on leaving this good earth anytime soon, but when the time comes, know that my love will remain with you through the rest of your days. Love just carries on, and on, and on. I don't hold back love anymore—I have become profligate, indiscriminate. The unguarded face of love—I know how it blesses whenever it appears.

I'm here, my darling—I'm carrying you so tenderly in my heart. You will find your way—this I know.

Love always and ever,

Mother

Nana

IN THE PHOTO our grandmother, Nana, is dressed in black, a black straw hat perched firmly on her head, her shoulders squared, her chin raised. Her left hand rests upon my shoulder— I am eleven—her right arm is around Bobby Ray, who would have been nine. He has on a jacket and tie, the tie a bit skewed, I am in my puffy pink dressy dress, both of us looking lost and forlorn, which we were. Uncle Gene posed us, snapped the picture on the day of the service.

The neighbors came loaded down with a big spread of food— fried chicken, potato salad, black-eyed peas and ham hock, sliced tomatoes and cantaloupe from their gardens. They brought apple pie, peach pie, a pound cake. Judy Stedman brought stuffed eggs on a plastic plate picturing a large American flag, red, white, and blue. Funny how you remember those little things.

Bobby Ray and I are looking at family photos, remembering.

Nana was past seventy when she got us—two more children to raise after a van went out of control, crossed the center line on the Minden Road and took both our parents. There were days when there was only one egg in the house, and Big Papa got that one, we children and Nana ate biscuits and syrup. Papa used to say, I wouldn't take a million dollars for you children, but I wouldn't take a plugged nickel for two more just like you. I think he meant that as a compliment. Nana never complained about us crowding the little house with its one tiny bathroom, no, we were made to feel the house was our home. She made my school dresses on the old Singer sewing machine, her foot moving up and down on the treadle, the needle singing on the seams.

We're grown now, back home for Nana's funeral. Big Papa died two years back, so now the house is going to be sold—I've heard the aunts whispering about it. It's our home too, but we don't own it, of course, it's not ours to claim. They are talking about what they want, in the way of furniture and knick-knacks. Nana had a fine collection of porcelain birds—Big Papa gave her a new one every Christmas. There's the sterling that we used on holidays, and the china with the roses that Aunt Bernadine sent Nana from Washington State.

The neighbors come streaming in again, same as before—not one moved in the twelve years we lived there: the Gerhardt sisters with their long braids wound around their heads; old Mr. and Mrs. Wilson, who sat and rocked on their front porch each evening; Mamie and Mike, who gave us pecans off their big tree; the widow Chrisler, moving more slowly now but still just as chatty as ever. We knew them all, knew their dogs too, they knew ours, the way it is in a little Southern town. They bring food again, only this time it's just after Christmas, there's fruit cake, lots of sliced turkey and cornbread dressing, pumpkin and mince pie.

Aunt Bernadine sits me down, asks, What do you want to take, Barbara Ann? I say I don't know, but then I say I want Nana's Bible. Nana read out loud every day from that big black Bible, rocking in her big blue over-stuffed rocking chair. Nana said that the Lord never puts on us more than we can stand. I didn't know what she meant then, but I do now. Bobby Ray says he wanted one of the quilts Nana made, though all of them are old from use, ragged from washing. Aunt Bernadine says, Go ahead and pick one, honey, and he did—the Rose of Sharon, the prettiest one of all.

We leave the next day, Bobby Ray and I, me with the Bible, him with the quilt. That is all we have from the home we grew up in, the rest will be parsed out and sold.

It is more than enough.

Death Catches Up with Us

Ready or not, here death comes, always on its own schedule, not ours. We may be ready, often are not, for in our culture we fail to acknowledge the reality of death. Too many of us choose to take our own lives, either overtly or by neglect, and we wonder at the level of despair in this wealthiest of countries. Currently, there is interest in learning to better negotiate our own dying and the dying of those we love.

Ways I Don't Want to Die

— Skiing into a tree while on a tryst with my married lover.

— Showing a friend how to use my unloaded handgun.

— Climbing a mountain "because it's there."

— Misremembering the rhyme to identify a coral snake. It's "Red touches yellow, kills a fellow" not "Red touches black, it will attack."

— Saying "I will, if you will" in any given situation.

— Stepping off a cliff while trying to get a great selfie to send to my girlfriend, at home with the flu.

— Choosing the Bates Motel as a refuge in a rainstorm.

— Using hair spray to stop the attack of a grizzly bear, mistaking it for a can of mace.

— Attempting to pet a wild chimpanzee after a superficial reading of Jane Goodall.

— Believing anyone, anytime, before any activity, who says to me, "This is absolutely safe."

— Being the only recorded individual who lets go of the rope during an Outward Bound exercise, finding myself downward bound.
— Reassuring my friends, who are frantically leaving the water, "I think I know a dolphin when I see one."

The Visitor

WAS THAT A knock at the door? She wasn't sure. She opened the door a crack, saw a pleasant-looking man standing there surrounded by an inordinate amount of light. Though she didn't know him, she felt absolutely safe. She invited him in.

Would you like a cup of tea? she offered.

No, he said.

A piece of pound cake then? It's just out of the oven.

No, thank you. I've come for you.

Oh, I see, she said. I've been expecting you for some time now. But this is a bit of a surprise. I was planning a movie this evening, I guess that's off.

I'm afraid so.

I'll get my things together.

What things?

Oh, family pictures, my wedding ring, a letter my father sent just before he died. And of course my iPhone.

You won't need any of that—most particularly, you won't need the phone.

I'm never without it.

Trust me, you won't need the phone.

Where exactly are we going?

It's not a place, it's another dimension entirely.

What do you mean?

He paused, considering how to answer her. He said, Do you remember that day last winter when big soft flakes of snow began wafting past the windows of your breakfast room? Remember how the little brown birds danced and played in the snow?

Yes, yes, I do remember.

Do you remember that suddenly you felt connected with the snow, the birds, felt connected with everything, everyone? Remember that you felt everything was perfect, just as it was? Remember your sense of absolute peace?

Yes, it was . . . extraordinary. I didn't . . . couldn't . . . understand. I've never told anyone.

Well, where you're going, that's what it's like.

What about the others, the ones left behind? I wanted to go to my granddaughter's wedding next Saturday. I wouldn't want to miss that. Couldn't you and I postpone our trip?

Sorry, but you're on the schedule for today. Don't worry about the wedding, you'll be there. This is how it will play out: your granddaughter will be devastated when she hears you are gone, she'll briefly consider postponing the wedding, then understand that you would not want that. She will include in the ceremony the lighting of a special candle to represent your presence, when the candle is lit, she will know you are with her, and will always be with her. That knowing will be as real as the scent of roses in her bouquet. The ritual of the candle lighting will cause the wedding guests to recall those dear ones gone from their lives, but who remain, somehow more present than when they were on earth. People will find unshed tears finally falling, they will not understand why they are so moved. At the reception people will say to one another, What a special ceremony, how full of love! Family members who have not spoken for years—including your granddaughter's mother and father, will turn kindly to one another, remark on the beauty of the ceremony, the loveliness of the bride, the promises made. They will remember the promises as yet unfulfilled in their own lives, yet will have no regrets.

I see, she said. That sounds all right.

It's hard to explain. I can only say you will be complete, whole, entirely without need. Are you ready to cross over?

Wait! There are things left unsaid, people to thank . . . people to forgive, yes, especially that. I want to say goodbye.

I'm sorry, but your name has been called, your time here is done. Do not be concerned, all is well.

What do you mean? All is not well. All has never been well.

Soon you will see with new eyes, you will understand that love is infinite, that mercy has no boundaries. Not one will fail. Not one will be left behind.

I don't understand.

I know. Just trust what I am saying.

I guess I don't have many options.

You can trust or not trust, it's all the same. Not one will be separate from another, all will be gathered together, all will be well.

She began to feel a deep sense of calm, not entirely of her volition. She remembered how it was when the snow fell and the birds played. She remembered her own wedding day, her mother's face, her father's firm arm as he escorted her down the aisle, the tears in his eyes. She remembered the first time she took her newborn son into her arms, the touch of her husband's hand the night he died.

The room filled with brilliant light. I'm ready now, she said, and gave him her hand.

A History of Her (Very Short) Sex Life

I know my daughter, I know my daughter . . . I don't know my daughter.

SHE IS THE firstborn child to a mother who is an artist, a father who is a professor. They are tenderly in love. She floats at ease in her mother's belly before being thrust into the world.

She is held in turn by a vast army of extended family members, she learns to trust love.

She lies in her baby bed as a toddler, as she falls asleep, hears laughter from the next room, her parents are making love.

She goes to kindergarten, notices that little boys and little girls are different, in their bodies and in their play.

She enters elementary school, where she makes valentines, gives them to her classmates, both boys and girls, hopes she will receive many, she does.

She is invited by her maternal grandfather to get an ice cream sundae in a shop that resembles a carousel. She is nine, likes the sundae very much, especially the whipped cream and the cherry. After they leave, her grandfather takes her to his small, dark apartment, lays her on the bed, pulls down her panties, touches her private parts. He makes grunting, satisfied sounds. She does not understand why he touches her this way. He continues to take her on outings most Saturdays throughout the summer and fall, always followed by a trip to his apartment. She knows something is wrong, she tells her mother she doesn't want to go for sundaes any more with her grandfather, she doesn't tell her mother why, her mother doesn't ask why. She never tells anyone about her grandfather's touching her, she fears terrible violence will come to her family if she does.

She enters junior high school, develops early, boys notice her, stare at the soft curves of her breasts. She begins to wear revealing clothing to get the attention of her classmates, both boys and girls, she dyes her light brown hair black. Her parents, dismayed at this turn of events, say to each other, it could be worse, at least she hasn't gotten a tattoo. She goes to a sex ed class where she learns about fallopian tubes and sperm, her teacher gives each girl a condom to fill with water, which they think is hilarious.

She gets a crush on Cheryl, a pretty girl a year older. They form a secret club of five girls who meet on Saturday mornings in a derelict building, they talk about many things, mostly about boys, they kiss and make promises to love one another forever. They leave the club behind in a year or so, not before getting heart tattoos on the nape of their neck, bonding them as sisters.

She attracts the attention of older boys when she enters high school. She likes a junior named Mike best. He takes her for ice cream, they make out. They continue to see each other against her parents' wishes, they say Mike is not the boy for her, he comes from a bad family, she doesn't care.

She takes Mike to the derelict building one Saturday morning, where they have sex among the ruined timbers and broken glass, she for the first time. She doesn't like the sex, it hurts, is pleased that Mike does. They continue to have sex every Saturday, except when Mike has football practice. The sex is fast, Mike is awkward and rough, she doesn't mind, she likes him.

She goes to the derelict building one Saturday, Mike doesn't show up. She texts him, he doesn't answer, texts him repeatedly: whr wur u? Mike texts her back, tells her his dad made him mow the lawn. She hears from her girlfriend that Mike is seeing someone else, she is distraught. She texts him, asks if this is so, he doesn't answer, she texts him three more times: is it tru??? he doesn't answer, she calls his cell, he answers. She asks, Are you seeing someone, tell me the truth. He doesn't speak, then says, Yes.

She retreats to her room, cries all day. Her parents ask what is wrong, nothing, go away, she says. They say to each other, just adolescent angst, all teens go through it. They withdraw, go about their business.

She gets a text from Matt, another football player. He asks her if she wants to hang out at the mall on Saturday, maybe get some pizza. At first she says no, but then thinking this would serve Mike right, she says yes. Matt buys her a Cinnabun at the mall, they walk around and talk, he holds her hand, she feels comforted. He says, I have my dad's car, let's go for a ride. They drive out to a little grove of trees about three miles from town, Matt stops the car, gets a blanket out of the trunk, spreads it on the grass. Let's have a picnic, he says, and grins. We don't have anything to eat, she says. We have this, Matt says, pulls out the flask his father takes to ball games, she giggles, reaches for the flask. The whiskey burns, then makes her feel warm inside, they continue to drink, Matt tells her that he has always wanted to get with her, she is so hot. She says, Do you want to see something, he says, Sure, she lifts her long hair from her neck, shows him the tattoo of the heart, he kisses the heart, he kisses her again and again, reaches up under her sweater, the whiskey makes her giggle, they have sex. When he enters her, she imagines she is with Mike. She likes the sex.

She hopes that Mike will text her, or call. He doesn't. She sees him at school with Sally, he is looking at Sally and grinning, he places his hand on Sally's shoulder, draws her to him. She texts Mike, asks R U Cing Sally? Mike doesn't answer, she texts again, U ned 2 ansr me!! he texts back, Yes, lev me B, it's ovr, U and me.

She refuses to go to school, her parents take her to a counselor, who asks her why she has begun cutting herself, she says, To make me feel something. The counselor tells her she is being self-destructive, which she already knows.

She gets a text from Matt: I wnt 2 CU agin—RU up fr tht? She texts back, I dn't no, he answers, I mis U, she texts OK, whre? She and Matt continue to have sex at least one a week, he doesn't hang out with her at school, there he is cool and distant, she thinks he doesn't want to make Mike mad for dating his ex. Then she sees Cheryl, now one of the cheerleaders, throw her arms around Matt after the football game, as he is coming off the field, he lifts her off the ground and holds her.

She goes home from the game and texts Cheryl, R U seeing Matt? he's my b-frnd, Cheryl doesn't answer, she texts again, R U??? Cheryl texts, Yes, so what, slut.

That night she locks herself in her room. She cuts her wrists again, this time deeply. She watches the blood flow, she thinks the crimson color is beautiful, her wrists seem to be someone else's wrists, the blood someone else's, she is just watching.

Her mother calls her to breakfast the following morning, then calls her louder, finally bangs on her daughter's door. Her daughter doesn't answer. She can't.

Not the Kind of Man

KEITH WAS NOT the kind of man you expect to be dying. He was thirty-three, the age Jesus was when he was crucified. Way, way too young.

He was handsome in that lanky basketball player kind of way, a head of thick dark hair, brown eyes that looked right through you—he sang in the church choir, joy all over his face. He was in fact, dying though—one of those cruel out-of-control cancers that can't wait for old age, the kind of disease that makes you doubt the existence of God, at least a god who gives a damn.

I'm Keith's minister—at least, I *was*—hard to think of him as dead. So Keith asks me to come to his home, gives me a cup of tea, and says, I want to be baptized. *Baptized?* He was a Unitarian Universalist, we don't . . . *baptize*, we *bless* babies, or at most *christen* them, we never, never baptize. It seems Keith was brought up Southern Baptist, but never went under the cleansing water, as his minister had urged him to. Most of his high school friends were saved at the spring revivals and baptized the following Sunday, coming up out of the baptismal font looking like wet puppies, but Keith never could "accept Jesus as his Lord and savior"—that decision had to be deep and true, he knew, and his heart registered a kind of stony silence when the choir sang "softly and tenderly, Jesus is calling, calling oh sinner, come home."

Now Keith and I had a history. After hearing me preach seven years, he came to my office to speak to me. He was angry. He said, You're always using women's poetry, female images, always telling stories about women. I feel left out.

I was taken aback. Maybe he was right, I thought, after all I am a woman, I tell stories about birthing, never about football. I did not remind Keith that since the founding of our church in 1866, congregants heard every sermon from a male perspective, had heard readings almost exclusively from male writers, ancient and modern—he hadn't arrived at my office to hear a lecture on feminism. So I told him I didn't realize how heavily I was leaning on female sources, promised him I would try to become more aware, as in fact I did.

I asked Keith why he wanted to be baptized. He explained that he wanted "to be sure" that he had not left undone a ritual that would keep him from whatever afterlife there might be. Having been raised Southern Baptist myself, I knew the feeling of being condemned to hell, remembered as a young adult in New Orleans being stopped by a street preacher with a wild look in his eyes who asked, *Are you saved*? I choked out a pathetic *I don't know*, before walking on, shaken.

I brought my grandmother's Bible with me that day. For some reason, long before I considered ministry—and though she had seven children and scores of grandchildren—I was the one given her Bible when she died. I also brought a vial of holy water given to me by my spiritual director, a nun, who brought it back from some saint's gravesite. A magician needs appurtenances.

I asked, *Do you, Keith Nelson Thompson, my brother, desire to receive this rite as a sign of your fellowship in the beloved community of faithful souls and as a mark of your partnership in the labors and comforts of the Christian life?*

Keith answered, *I do.*

Touching the holy water to his forehead, I said, *I baptize you in the name of the Father, the Son, and the Holy Spirit.* Then I threw in my own bit: *Through this public commitment, Keith, you have made known what has been present within you for many long years, a giving over of yourself to the Holy and an understanding that you are held now and will be held forever in the everlasting arms.*

Who was I, reject from the Catholics at twelve for my questions and reject from the Southern Baptists at thirty-five for my divorce, to baptize anyone? Would this ritual "take" or not?

I recalled, then, the words of a seminary professor. Two weeks before my ordination was to take place, I entered his office distraught. I said, I don't know if I'm good enough to be a minister. Having always been a "good girl," I didn't have any colorful sins to confess, for I was the straightest of straight arrows. But I knew after ordination I would be held to the highest standards. I knew myself to be judgmental, pious, arrogant—those soul-killing sins that separate a person from God. Could I be loving enough, generous enough? Besides, I had never been a fan of sacrifice, now the crucifix and the bleeding Jesus hung over me.

The professor was elderly, slow to speak. My breath turned shallow, I waited. Finally, he spoke. He said, Remember that the efficacy of the sacrament is not determined by the purity of the celebrant.

I got it. The ministry is not about me. I was just offering myself, in all my moral frailty, to be a vessel.

So yes, it was a makeshift baptism, no robes, no immersion, no witness but my own. And yet that day I had no doubt that whatever gods may be would look with favor upon Keith.

Mercy and Truth Have Met Together

We tremble before making our choice in life, and after having made it again tremble in fear of having chosen wrong. But the moment comes when our eyes are opened, and we see and realize that grace is infinite. . . . See! That which we have chosen is given us, and that we have refused is, also and at the same time, granted us. Ay, that which we have rejected is poured upon us abundantly. For mercy and truth have met together and righteousness and bliss have kissed one another!

—*Isak Dinesen,* Babette's Feast

MARY HAD ALREADY flunked hospice twice, twice living past her allotted six months, this time she'll make it, she thought. She felt herself withdrawing from visitors, who meant well but chatted endlessly about things she cared nothing for; from her lifelong habit of saving the world from its own foolishness; from her husband's reassurances and queries about her well-being; from the duty to look presentable for whoever walked through the door of her hospital room; from food, the most dependable source of pleasure throughout her life. She drifted in and out of consciousness, dreaming yet not quite dreaming, visited by phantoms, fragments.

— her two-year-old self sitting by the bed of her sleeping father, playing with his belt
— her mother chopping carrots
— her first-grade teacher, Miss Elliot, saying, Mary, turkeys are not blue now, are they
— the taste of the wafer at her First Communion, the gold of the priest's garments
— her fall from the slide, the cut on her chin
— her friend Lucy, who moved away the summer before the sixth grade
— the starfish that washed ashore on the beach at Sanibel Island
— her father's eyes the day he left for good
— her dog Trixie racing for the ball, then lying still in the street
— the blue dress with sparkles she wore to the prom
— her first love, the boy with the yellow hair and glasses who sat beside her in band
— the table set with her grandmother's china at Thanksgiving
— her husband-to-be proposing in the restaurant, laughter rising all around them
— the red fox running on the side of the road

— the light flickering from the flames engulfing the kitchen, the race out
— the snowstorm making her world white
— the blue heron rising suddenly from the creek

She saw all that she was, all that the years had taken, all the possibilities, all the refusals, all the gifts. She knew all was as it should be.

Mary was jolted awake—Nurse Sarah coming in with ice cream for her. They only had vanilla, Sarah said.

My favorite! said Mary, as she reached for it. She picked up the spoon, lifted the sweetness to her lips. She thought nothing had ever tasted better.

The Meaning of Life

Through the ages, philosophers, theologians, artists, and writers have attempted to answer this question of meaning. Humans are meaning-makers. The consumerist culture of our society is seductive though, and so we struggle to find meaning beyond getting and spending. When we come to the end of our allotted time, which values will have emerged as primary?

To fail to reflect upon the meaning of our lives will leave us traveling through our days responding to whatever the environment offers up, and so leave life asking why we wasted so much of our precious time.

What We Have Left

ON SATURDAY, January 13, 2018, IPAWS (Integrated Public Alert System) sent a message to citizens and visitors in Hawaii:

> ## EMERGENCY ALERT
> Ballistic missile threat inbound to Hawaii.
> Seek immediate shelter. This is not a drill.

—Drivers got out of their cars and stared at the sky.

—Kevin Dean told his wife, "Head to the school. Get the kids!" She said, "What are we going to do about the cats?"

—Chauncey Miller went to the airport and tried to book a flight out of Hawaii.

—Caleb Jones, an AP writer, jumped into his car and headed for the hills, hoping to escape the damage at ground zero. He reported people driving extremely fast from the center of Honolulu, using their cell phones as they drove.

—People crawled under restaurant tables.

—One little girl was lowered into a manhole.

—5,500 people called 911.

—A man googled "safety nuclear bomb how shelter" and was told to get inside.

—Tourists were "herded like cows" into the basement of a hotel.

—One man had family members in various places. He had to choose with whom to spend his last hours on earth. Later he texted, "I chose to go home to two little ones, was tearing up South Street to the freeway when I heard it was a mistake. F— you, Hawaii Civil Defense."

—Julie Hollenbeck was at the Sheraton Maui. She went to the lobby, where she saw "groups of people in their swimsuits and little coverups, holding drinks, terrified."

—Nichole Cruz was at the Maui Coast Hotel. She thought to herself, *This is how you're going to die—in a place that's paradise.*

—John Peterson, a golfer participating in the U.S. PGA Tour's Sony Open, hid with his wife and children under mattresses in the bathtub.

—Amanda Thompson and her husband threw supplies—blankets, diapers, food, water—into a tiny closet under the stairs of their home and huddled there with their infant and two-year-old.

—A man texted his family: "I love you. I don't know if this is it, or if I get to see you again, but I just wanted you to know, if this was the last time we talked, I love you all." He said later, "You have to say that, don't you?"

—Mike Staskow, a retired military captain, remembered: "I was running through all the scenarios in my head, but there was nowhere to go."

When people think they are going to die, they fall into an instinctual response. The brain signals the autonomous nervous system, heart rate and blood pressure increase, and breathing quickens. People try to find protection. They try to get information.

Sometimes, though, there's nowhere to go. In the end they connect however they can with family and friends. They draw together and hold one another. They understand that all they have left, all they've really ever had, is love.

Things They Will Not Say About Me in My Obituary But I Wish They Would

She was a true people person.
She was a super cook and hosted many
    Thanksgiving dinners.
Her greatest pleasure in life was being with
    her grandchildren.
She always had a smile on her face.
She never lost her optimistic, positive
    attitude.
She was above all a devoted wife and mother.
She could see the beauty in everyone.
She LOVED Christmas.
She literally smiled through her trials.
She had a servant's heart.
She will be missed by everyone who knew her.

Love Letters from God

I cried out, Where are you, God?
And God sent only questions:
When you visit your brother's house, does he
   hide the key?
Have you noticed how the rose opens to the sun?
Why sleep in a bed of fear?
Do you know the difference between a judge and
   a lover?
Who is that knocking on your door?
Can't we just be friends?

The Exorcist

CHARLOTTE noticed something strange happening in her closet—her clothing was beginning to multiply.

Charlotte dresses well. Designer dresses, bags, shoes. She favors linen pants and skirts, silk blouses—a classy combination. As she was getting dressed for a party, she noticed that instead of two white silk blouses, she had four, two of them identical. Hmmmm, she said. She reached for a pair of black pants, found that instead of four she had six. She didn't remember buying them. In fact, she was sure she had not. She began to get a slight headache.

She checked her sweater drawer, counted a total of twenty-five sweaters of various colors, instead of the eighteen she remembered. She had fifteen belts instead of twelve. She often wore hand-knitted shawls, treasuring these for she felt they complemented any outfit. She was shocked when she opened her drawer of shawls only to find two new ones: a blue shawl with silver threads and a black one, neither of which had ever been worn. The same phenomenon was occurring with her jackets. She checked her original twelve and found she had sixteen.

Charlotte could only conclude that her clothing was replicating itself! Something inexplicable and frightening is happening, she thought, something *demonic*, a kind of Rosemary's baby in the closet. What to do? Who could she ask for help? She decided to call her parish priest.

Father Klein didn't believe Charlotte at first, implying that she had no doubt purchased the clothing, then forgot about it. He said that happens, not to worry, he knows other well-to-do parishioners who have the same problem. But she persisted. Evil is stalking my closet! she said. At his wit's end, he referred her to an exorcist, Brother Paul.

Charlotte called right away for an appointment. Exorcists have appointments, Father Klein told her, like a therapist or spiritual director. They also will come to your home in case of an emergency, which Charlotte thought aptly described her situation. She had become terrified to look into her closet, or even enter her house, so she spent the night with her sister, who was unsympathetic. She thought Charlotte was cracking up.

Brother Paul met Charlotte outside her house the very next evening. You would never know he was a professional exorcist, she thought—he was a shaggy, worn-looking man in his sixties, with a bit of stubble—not at all priest-like. He wore baggy jeans, a T-shirt with a Nike swoosh on it, both garments looking like last-day purchases from a yard sale. A tattoo of a cross was on his left hand, a snake on his right, he wore Doc Marten boots. He arrived with only a flask of holy water—no other tools of the trade, no special robes. Charlotte asked him about his fee. No charge, he said—exorcists do these purification rituals gratis. He said the ability to engage the demonic is considered a special gift from God, and an exorcist would never traffic in commerce. Well, the price is certainly right, Charlotte thought, and she agreed to try his services.

Charlotte told Brother Paul, the thing is, I am not religious in any way. He said it didn't matter. He was the officiant, he said, and the one responsible for performing the rites and confronting the demon. He did say he had never heard of this kind of problem, but readily agreed that self-replicating clothing is undoubtedly demonic. He told Charlotte she must do exactly as he directed.

He asked her to remove all her clothes from hangers and from drawers where they were stored, and to place the garments side-by-side all over the floors of her home. Soon every inch of floor was filled with clothing. She had to include shoes, too, he said, and Charlotte had more than fifty pairs of those. Purses, of course, all fifty-five of them. Literally hundreds of hats and scarves. Not to mention the jackets and coats. Charlotte's beautifully appointed home became a vast sea of clothing, a sea of many colors, rolling and undulating throughout the floor space. She figured this exorcism was going to be one big waste of time, but she decided to play it out.

The exorcist began his incantations in Latin—then he walked about on the clothing in his boots, sprinkling holy water as he moved from room to room. Whenever a drop of water struck a garment or a purse or a shoe, it disappeared. Charlotte was amazed! Within half an hour, the items were gone, the floor was bare, her closet empty. As a last gesture, Brother Paul sprinkled Charlotte with holy water, a baptism of sorts, and she found herself without clothing or shoes! He then handed her a simple coarsely woven robe and some leather sandals.

You are fortunate, he said. The demon has left. One caveat, though. You must wear this brown robe and these sandals for one year, and nothing else. Otherwise, the demon will return.

I can't do that! Charlotte protested. I work, I have a social life. I can't wear this stupid brown robe! Brown is not even on my color chart. What will people think?

Exactly, he said. And walked out the door.

Eclipse

a true story of the greatest racehorse
of all time

NO DOUBT you've never heard of Eclipse, the greatest race horse that ever lived. He was a chestnut, with a narrow blaze running down his face, and big for his time—just over sixteen hands—and had a difficult temperament. His first race, on May 3, 1767, consisted of three heats of four miles each. It was an easy win. Eclipse went on to win eighteen races, easily besting all contenders. He was retired to stud after a racing career of about seventeen months, because nobody would bet on any other horse. It has been estimated that 95 percent of today's thoroughbreds, or nearly every living thoroughbred, has something of Eclipse in their pedigree.

A few years ago, scientists from the Royal Veterinary College in London decided to study Eclipse, to understand why he was so fast. The researchers took a DNA sample from one of his teeth. They studied paintings of the horse and read reports of his races. They analyzed Eclipse's skeleton and developed models of his movement. They reconstructed one of his legs and built theoretical limbs on a computer. When the study was done, they came to the dubious conclusion that Eclipse's extraordinary speed was due to his "averageness." His legs were not too short and not too long.

"Horsefeathers," declared Dr. James Rooney, an expert in equine biomechanics at the University of Kentucky. He said that the scientists based their conclusions solely on Eclipse's skeletal structure and missed the fundamental factor. "There's one thing they don't know about this horse: what his attitude was," Dr. Rooney said. "Some of the sorriest, worst-looking horses have been great racehorses."

We are left with what was written on a card at the time of Eclipse's death: "His heart, like his legend, was large."

Why I Don't Tidy

TIDYING is a big craze now—given all the junk we consumers accumulate, it's a concept whose time has come. The basic instruction is to touch every item in your home and ask yourself, Does this bring me joy? If not, get rid of it. It sounds so simple, so straightforward, so . . . responsible. I jumped right in.

I thought I would start with books. I found the decision-making excruciating. Should I keep Jung or Freud? Galway Kinnell or Louise Glück? *Lord of the Flies* or *Lord Jim*? Should I keep all of my two thousand books—or none of them? They are wise and faithful friends, always there when I need them. For example, now would be an excellent time to get a hit from Walt Whitman. Applying the standard "what brings me joy," I would say unequivocally, all my books, with the possible exception of the following: *Six Easy Pieces: Essentials of Physics Explained by Its Most Brilliant Teacher* by Richard Feynman, which I started three times, but never got past page 4, where I learned "all things are made of atoms, little particles that move around";

Radical Acceptance: Embracing Your Life, a goal which I've given up on as unrealistic; and *Always Hungry? Retrain Your Fat Cells & Lose Weight Permanently*, which describes a system that requires at least four hours of planning and shopping and cooking each day, and in addition, would require me to give up Diet Coke and movie popcorn, my only reliable sources of comfort and tranquility outside of my tranquilizers. Actually, when I bought the book I misread the subtitle as *Retain Your Fat Cells & Lose Weight Permanently*.

Another troubling consequence of tidying would be giving up gifts I have been given by people I love who have no comprehension of my taste or sensibilities. A short list would include a candle in a classic tin labeled Pure Maple Syrup, which when lighted smells like maple syrup, sent to me by an old friend who lives in Vermont; a quite large pencil sketch of a dying tulip, framed and given to me by my son before he dropped out of art school; a parrot alarm clock from a dear friend whose last name is Polly—get it? The clock awakens the sleeper with a parrot's raucous cry, Awk, awk, get up! Get up!

My greatest dilemma, though, is the time commitment that tidying requires. If I were to touch every book I owned, every item of clothing, every item of décor in my house, I would probably need a year of full-time work to get the job done. Tidying began to slip down my list of urgent priorities. I could not allow tidying to take over my cluttered but all-too-brief life, only to further clutter it with tidying.

So I've decided just to keep my belongings at bay until I die, thus cleverly passing on this job to my children, who will doubtless need something mindless to do while they are processing their grief.

Poesy

A river running deep with rain
a dive from the high board
a blackbird with a red wing
a lace curtain trembling at an open window
an old doll with blue eyes, startled
a pair of shoes polished, tucked under a child's bed
a cathedral bell at dusk
a pencil clutched by a boy learning his letters
a blue heron's nest, black, in the skeleton of a tree
a seat on a city bus, left warm by the previous occupant
a hand-knitted sock with three dropped stitches
an apron, flowered, made from a feed sack
a glimmer of lightning scratching open the night sky

What Is the Question?

based on a story attributed to Rev. Harry Scholefield

AT A DINNER for interfaith leaders, the dean of the local Episcopal diocese found himself seated next to a Buddhist teacher. The salad arrived, the rolls were passed, the dinner came, finally dessert and coffee were served, and the teacher sat quietly through it all. The priest, who was sociable and had the best of manners, resolved to draw in the teacher. *Maybe he is just uncomfortable, being among so many Christians*, he thought. But he was uncertain as to how to open a conversation with a man who seemed so self-contained. Finally, the priest turned toward the teacher and said, "I've always wondered—who do you think Jesus is?"

The teacher nodded and smiled, but remained silent. The priest thought, what with the chatter and clinking of glass and silver, maybe this man didn't hear the question. So he turned again to the teacher and in a somewhat louder voice, though still within the bounds of decorum, said, "I'm curious—who do you think Jesus is?"

The teacher put down his fork, touched the linen napkin to his lips, then spoke: "The question is, who do you think you are?"

How We Remember Them

THE FOLLOWING are excerpts from obituaries in the *Oregonian*. The survivors who write these accounts say in a few words what they remember. We read about the accomplishments of those who have departed, but more often what remains is the everydayness of their lives, the uniqueness of their personalities.

Jerry, 70

His putting was incredibly accurate.

Ross, 95

Almost every day of his life, he relished several cups of good coffee and at least one heaping bowl of ice cream.

Robert, 84

Bob enjoyed playing his piano. The neighbors would ask him to open his windows so they could listen.

Stephanie, 44

Stephanie donned her blingiest earrings, climbed on her scooter, and zoomed up to heaven on Labor Day, heartbreakingly unexpectedly.

Ronald, 84

He was known for his crazy Christmas outfits and his "quack, quack, quack" as he entered the room.

Evelyn, 91

Her hobbies were walking, lawn bowling, and Bunco.

John, 77

The family asks that you keep John in your prayers and root just a little bit more for the Beavers.

Siobain, 49

Siobain's presence and her beautiful smile would light up a room, even when she arrived a bit late.

Kurt, 45

In a card he sent in the week before his death, Kurt wrote, "I know Beauty will continue to unfold. I know Love will flourish. And I know we must gruel sometimes to get our joy. P.S. Never used gruel as a verb before. Works."

Diane, 48

The world will never be the same because the Diane-shaped piece is missing.

David, 92

David lost an arm in an accident while in his twenties, but he quickly adapted and could do just about anything with one arm, including waterskiing, tying shoes, and building and flying RC model airplanes.

Orville, 82

Orville passed away in Portland, with no family or friends to claim him. He served honorably in the U.S. Coast Guard during the Korean War era. A graveside service with military honors will be held. Arrangements are in the care of the Dignity Memorial Homeless Veteran Burial Program.

Barbara, 87

The week before she died, her lifelong friend, Betty Weeks, counseled her to "take each day and count your blessings." Mom heard that as "count your breakfasts." The family took that to heart and had a memorial breakfast in her memory.

Patrick, 67

His black Labrador, Sequoia, waits for him at the door.

Edna, 97

Edna was a lifelong follower of Jesus, and her family is rejoicing in the hope that she is now serving warm Swedish coffeecake to all her friends in heaven.

James, 67

In his twenties, he hitchhiked from New York to San Francisco in two days and was sure that he held the unofficial cross-country hitchhiking record.

Andrew, 70

He was proudest of his membership in Thacher's Silver Dollar Club. He earned that honor by scooping up a silver dollar from the ground while cantering by on his beloved horse, Bandit.

Mabel, 95

She and Dale had their last dance together just three weeks before her passing. They danced to "Waltzing with the Angels."

Robert, 65

He lived in Seattle and enjoyed Eastern philosophies, marksmanship, and repairing muscle cars.

Phyllis, 94

Even though Alzheimer's disease took much of Mom's memory, almost at the end she was heard to regale us with her OSU loyalty: "A Beaver born, a Beaver bred and when I die, I'll be a Beaver dead."

Rose, 99

She lived in Portland most of her life, except for the time she spent in the Minidoka concentration camp in Idaho for over three years.

Russell, 66

He will be fondly remembered for his bounding laughter, brilliant blue eyes, and eccentric taste in shoes.

James, 92

Dad loved Tabasco sauce, which went on everything he ate.

Gerald, 83

Gary continued to love fishing to the very end, although it seemed most of the time all he caught was rocks.

Walt, 86

Walt was famous to his family and friends for his "Snicker-doodle Surprise" cookies that he loved to bake.

Colin, 52

He loved Mustang cars and had a collection of Matchbox cars and flashlights.

Bill, 86

He was chubby as a baby and was nicknamed "Skinny" by an uncle. The name stuck for the rest of his life. Bill became a garbage hauler in 1955 and collected discarded antique items.

Linda, 58

"Build Me Up Buttercup" was an all-time favorite, and she would nail the backup vocals every time.

Jo Ann, 89

Jo was an accomplished pianist, in the opinion of her eight children. When she wasn't changing diapers, doing laundry, or giving birth, Jo would play her favorite melodies on the piano.

Richard, 89

He gave twenty gallons of blood to the Red Cross.

Michael, 54

He was a small-business owner in Kent, Washington, and loved his family, work, clients, traveling, the Seahawks, and life.

We blame the Seahawks' lousy play call for Mike's untimely demise.

Gertrude, 82

Gertrude's known childhood really began at the early age of about one year old when she was admitted to the Veterans of Foreign Wars (VFW) Home for Children in Eaton Rapids, Michigan.

Jerry, 55

Jerry's generous heart stopped suddenly Jan. 23, 2015.

Lorraine, 79

Lorraine is well remembered and regarded as the "queen of the chicken dance."

Michael, 62

Michael had a life of service spanning more than forty years in the janitorial craft. In the face of adversity, you take life in stride and make the best of what you are given. Donations may be made to Stephen's Place, an outstanding home for special-needs adults.

Marguerite, 89

One thing mom always appreciated in reading the obituaries was the cause of death. "I know they died. Why else would they be here? It would just be nice to know how." So Mom for your obit, let's just say you were tired and worn out.

Charlie, 20 days

She was a beautiful baby girl who touched so many lives. During her brief stay with us, Charlie earned the nickname

"Bright Eyes" and brought smiles to all who met her. She loved being held in her mother's arms more than anything else.

Emma, 92

Most of all she loved making money.

Carole, 72

In 1984, Carole and Duncan McLeod were married. Duncan soon learned his place in the family pecking order: her daughter, the duck, the dog, and then Duncan.

Lillian, 97

Her childhood nickname was "Duchess," and she had that certain imperial "here I am, you lucky people" attitude her entire life.

Lorraine, 70

Lorraine went to as many dances as she could talk Jim into and spent almost as much time avoiding playing golf with him.

Christine, 64

In 1977, she married Michael, her best friend and soulmate. She and Michael volunteered with Meals on Wheels for many years.

Michael, 64

Michael passed away peacefully following several days of compassionate care at Salem Hospital. Michael and wife Chris's final "big adventure" was a recent 12,000-mile, six-week road trip which took them to thirty-eight states west to east. However, because they were organ donors, we are confident that their travels have continued.

Epilogue

Vocatus atque non vocatus deus aderit.

SOME PEOPLE are hard to love, others you can't help loving. Gayle fell into the latter category. A woman with red high heels and a smile wider than the sun, Gayle served as a greeter at the church. Sunday morning visitors succumbed to her warmth, her deep down, contagious joy.

So when she told me she had liver cancer, and was not long for this world, my heart took a hit. I went to visit her in the hospital after her surgery, to give what comfort I could. Her smile was intact. She let me know early in the visit that she was a humanist, that she did not believe in God, I'm guessing to fend off any God language I might lay on her, or prayer. I was fine with that, reluctant believer that I am.

So we ended up talking about old times—she had grown up AME (African Methodist Episcopal) in the deep South. I had grown up Southern Baptist. She said she had loved the singing in the church of her childhood, and missed the old hymns. Me, too, I said.

Do you know "In the Garden"? she asked.

That was my grandmother's favorite hymn! I said. My sister and I used to sing it together, she was soprano, me alto.

Do you want to sing it with me? she said. And so we sang, just the two of us. Actually, we sounded pretty good. Maybe because we sang with such heart.

> *And He walks with me, and He talks with me*
> *And He tells me I am His own*

I stayed longer than I usually stay on these sorts of calls. Gayle lifted my spirits, and I didn't want to leave. Finally I said my goodbyes, and we hugged. Gayle always hugged. She saw in my face, I suppose, that I didn't want to let her go. She said, smiling, but with quite a bit of firmness in her voice, "I'm going to be all right. I want you to know that." That was the last time we spoke.

William Blake wrote, "Joy and woe are woven fine." A truism I've learned well. As a minister, I have long witnessed human beings in this drama we call life. I have seen fear and grief *in extremis*, as people face betrayals of body and mind; losses of parents, spouses, children; dreams dashed and deferred. And up close, as I have been privileged to be, I have caught glimpses of courage and joy that are breathtaking, causing wonder to arise, and thankfulness.

Why this sudden arising of gratitude? I think it is the *holding* I sense, an undergirding of the whole of existence, that will not let us go. It is what brings both tears and laughter in memorial services. It is, at base, a reality undefined and often unacknowledged, that enables us to feel, in the midst of all that life throws at us, "All is well. All is well with my soul."

I could let Gayle go that day. Because of course I took her with me, and she is with me still. She is way beyond any tenet or belief. She is in the arms of Love.

Marilyn Sewell

Acknowledgments

I offer thanks

to Lydia Davis, whose work I stumbled across early in my process, and whose writing has been a constant source of inspiration.

to Kim Stafford, who taught me that stories can take an almost infinite variety of form.

to Jennifer Springsteen, who served as my editor on early drafts of this book, lending valuable advice and support.

to Katie Radditz, who read a draft of my manuscript, offering a warm and gentle critique.

to Margot Campbell Gross and Peter Gross, whose generous hospitality in their home included comments which helped me complete some malingering pieces.

to Barbara Wiley, who organized my first public reading of my stories at Gray's Landing. It was then that I began to believe my quirky little stories might be appealing to a broad audience.

to Mary Benard, my editor at Skinner House, who offered invaluable advice.

and most of all to George Crandall, my dear husband and partner, who served as a savvy and perceptive first reader. He has been indiscriminate in his love for me and supportive of my work.